DREAM WEAVER

A Hidden Falls Romance

Other books by Amanda Harte:

The *Hidden Falls* Romance Series:
The Brass Ring
Painted Ponies

The *War Brides* Trilogy:
Laughing at the Thunder
Whistling in the Dark
Dancing in the Rain

The *Unwanted Legacies* Romance Series:
Bluebonnet Spring
Strings Attached
Imperfect Together

Moonlight Masquerade

DREAM WEAVER

•

Amanda Harte

AVALON BOOKS
NEW YORK

Published by Thomas Bouregy & Co., Inc.
160 Madison Avenue, New York, NY 10016

Library of Congress Cataloging-in-Publication Data

Harte, Amanda.
    Dream weaver : a Hidden Falls romance / Amanda Harte.
        p. cm. — (Hidden Falls romance series)
    ISBN 978-0-8034-9832-7 (acid-free paper)
    I. Title.

PS3515.A79457D74 2007
813'.6—dc22

                                    200003743

PRINTED IN THE UNITED STATES OF AMERICA
ON ACID-FREE PAPER
BY HADDON CRAFTSMEN, BLOOMSBURG, PENNSYLVANIA

In memory of my father, Worth A. Bailey,
a wonderful storyteller and my first teacher.

When I started writing this book, I realized how much I didn't know about schools. It has, after all, been more than a few years since I graduated from high school. Fortunately for me, I had the assistance of three people who are experts in their fields. I'd like to thank:

Eileen List, a talented school librarian, for agreeing to serve as my primary reference, even though it meant responding to more emails than I'm sure she anticipated.

Kim Johnsen, a real life FCS teacher, who graciously answered a total stranger's questions and explained the challenges faced by modern day Family and Consumer Science teachers.

William Seyse, a man of many interests, who unraveled the mysteries of school consolidations and the politics behind them.

My heartfelt thanks go to each of them. Any mistakes are mine alone.

Chapter One

"**Y**ou need a husband."

Claire Conners drizzled syrup on her waffles, noting with satisfaction how the amber liquid complemented the delicately browned cakes she'd just made. At least one thing had gone well this morning. Though it was tempting to ignore her grandmother's comment by pleading an early morning meeting at school, that was the coward's way, and Claire was no coward. Besides, it would accomplish little. Glinda had a PhD in persistence.

Bowing to the inevitable, Claire asked, "Why do I need a husband?" Today, that is. Her grandmother had a seemingly endless supply of reasons Claire should be married.

As Glinda tipped her head forward, her trademark golden curls bounced, revealing gray roots. Claire considered trying to distract her with a reminder to call the beauty shop, but before she could speak, her grandmother produced today's excuse for matrimony. "You told me your car needed an oil change. A husband could do that."

It was vintage Glinda, insisting that any task could be best done by a husband. Claire tried not to sigh. There were dis-

1

advantages to living with a woman named after the Good Witch of the North, particularly when that woman believed her mission in life was to guide her granddaughter into a state of wedded bliss.

"Best Motors does great oil changes, and I don't have to cook dinner for them," Claire said as mildly as she could. "Speaking of which, I thought we'd have chicken crepes for dinner tonight." They were one of Glinda's favorite entrees, worthy, she claimed, of the good china and eating in the dining room rather than here in the kitchen.

Claire smiled as she looked at the blue-and-white gingham curtains and placemats, chosen to match the dress Judy Garland had worn when she played Dorothy. Thank goodness Glinda had not insisted on carrying the Wizard of Oz theme throughout the house. Claire preferred the polished hardwood floor to a yellow brick hallway.

"You're trying to change the subject, honey. It won't work." Glinda helped herself to another waffle. "You know how much I want to hold a great-grandchild." She had brought out the big guns, her argument of last resort.

Claire laid down her fork and faced her grandmother. "You know I love you dearly, Glinda. I'd do almost anything for you, but I am not going to marry someone I don't love just so you can have a great-grandchild." How many times did they have to have the same discussion? Claire pulled out her own heavy artillery. "Haven't you read the divorce statistics lately?" She glanced at her watch. Thank goodness, it was time to leave for school. When she got started on her favorite topic, Glinda could argue for an hour.

Glinda shook her head, refuting Claire's point. "People don't work at marriage any longer. They give up at the first problem."

"That may be true, but the fact is, I haven't met anyone who was worth the risk." Claire grabbed her bags.

"You're too fussy. You should take a risk."

"Good-bye, Glinda. We'll have asparagus with the crepes."

Ten minutes later Claire poured herself a cup of coffee in the faculty dining room. Though it was Friday and her students would fidget more than normal as they anticipated their two-day reprieve from classes, they'd be a welcome relief—her own reprieve—from Glinda's persistence.

"You look a tad stressed this morning," Ruby Baker told her.

Claire shrugged but managed a smile for her best friend. Half a foot shorter than Claire, Ruby's hair was a dozen shades lighter brown, her eyes a less vibrant blue. On bad days, Ruby would declare that she was a pale imitation of Claire; on good days, she admitted that looking like a pixie wasn't so bad.

"Glinda was on her soap box again."

Ruby reached for one of the donuts that were her downfall. "You should have taken my advice and moved in with me." Ever since her divorce, Ruby had tried to coax Claire into sharing her apartment.

"The idea is mighty tempting this morning," Claire admitted, "but I don't know how I'd handle the guilt if Glinda fell down the stairs or was sick. After all, she's almost seventy."

"And healthier than most people our age." Ruby grimaced at her donut, then took another bite.

"That's a valid point."

"Of course it is. I'm always right."

"And modest, too." Claire drained her coffee, then eyed the pot. There were two cups left. "Since neither of us has a date tomorrow, do you want to do something together?" she asked Ruby, after she'd decided to exhibit willpower and forgo a second infusion of caffeine.

"Movie and a dinner?" Ruby suggested.

"Why not? At least I won't have to cook." Claire frowned.

"I tried to bribe Glinda with her favorite dishes, but it didn't work. She kept up the litany of reasons I needed a husband."

"Let me guess. They were . . ."

Before Ruby could finish her sentence, Gerry Feltz's voice filled the room. "May I have your attention." The principal began his announcement the way he always did, causing teachers in the dining room to halt their conversations as they listened to the public address system. "There will be a mandatory meeting of all staff today at three thirty in the auditorium. Thank you, and have a good day."

"As if we will now," Ruby muttered. "What do you suppose that's all about?"

"Judging from his tone of voice, it's not good news."

It wasn't. Though there had been quiet speculation throughout the day, fueled by the fact that the school board meeting the previous evening had been closed to visitors, no one guessed the magnitude of the principal's announcement.

"There's no easy way to say this." Gerry sat on the edge of the stage, his furrowed brow confirming the fact that he was uncomfortable with whatever it was he had to tell them. "You've all seen the demographics. The boomlet kids will graduate next year. After that . . ." He shook his head. "There simply aren't enough students to sustain the school."

Claire took a deep breath. Like the other teachers, she and Ruby had been concerned about the dwindling class size. Perhaps they'd taken an ostrich-in-the-sand attitude, but they hadn't expected action to occur this quickly. "Rockledge and Bartonsville are in the same situation," Gerry continued. "We all agree that there's only one answer. Unless something changes, the school boards are recommending a regional high school, probably in Rockledge."

"But that's a half-hour bus ride each way," Claire pointed out. "It'll make for a long day for the kids."

Gerry nodded. "I don't like the idea any better than you do."

"When will we know for certain?" It was Ruby who asked the question that was foremost on everyone's mind.

"By the end of the summer. That will give us a year to get the new school built and work out all the details."

"Like who has jobs," Ruby said softly.

"It's not just us," Claire pointed out as she and Ruby joined the uncharacteristically quiet group filing out of the auditorium. "What about the kids? A bunch of them have after-school jobs to help their families make ends meet. The longer bus ride will mean fewer hours of work for them."

Ruby fumbled in her purse, searching for her keys. "Face it, Claire. This town has been on a steady downhill slide for decades. There's no future here."

"I don't want to believe that."

"Believe it. The reality is, it'll take a miracle to save Hidden Falls."

Claire shook her head slowly. "Glinda was wrong. I don't need a husband. I need a miracle worker."

"Moreland." John barked his name into the phone, wondering who was calling this early. Whoever it was had blocked caller ID. That was odd, as was the fact that anyone would phone at six thirty. Few knew that John came to work at what the rest of the staff considered a ridiculous hour.

"Good morning, handsome." The woman's melodic voice told him she was smiling.

"Angela! Where are you?"

"At the club. My cell is out of juice, so I'm using one of their phones." Her voice was slightly breathless, confirming her next words. "I was on the treadmill, and when I saw this, I just couldn't wait."

John's smile broadened as he heard the faint rustling of paper. It never ceased to amaze him that a woman as disorganized as Angela Stevenson could be so successful.

"Didn't you tell me that your family once lived in some godforsaken little town near Binghamton?" she asked.

"I don't recall describing it exactly that way," John said, "but my grandparents did live there until my father was around five. What triggered your interest in Hidden Falls, New York?" The town was one hundred and fifty miles and a light year away from the headquarters of JBM Enterprises with its breathtaking views of the Manhattan skyline. Why had Angela even introduced the subject?

"Because, my dear friend and treasured client, it appears that your ancestral estate is for sale . . . cheap."

"And precisely which part of that statement did you think would interest me?" He liked the "dear friend" part. They'd certainly dated often enough to be considered dear friends. As for the rest, there was no denying that Angela had made a small fortune out of commissions on John's real estate transactions. That probably qualified him for "treasured client" status. But the reference to his ancestral estate left him yawning.

"The cheap part. You could make a boat load of money. Oh, pardon me," she corrected herself, "you could achieve exorbitant rates of return if you worked your magic on it, restored it to its former glory, blah, blah, blah."

Had it been anyone other than Angela who had presented the preposterous proposal, John would have simply hung up the phone. Unfortunately, the fact that they were "dear friends" meant he couldn't do that to her. "Just who would buy the white elephant once my work was done?" John frowned, remembering his grandfather's stories. "The reason my grandparents left Hidden Falls was that they had to close the mill." In its heyday, Moreland Mills had been one of the premier textile factories in the country. That heyday was now ancient history. "Granddad knew that the town had no future." John continued, "Quite honestly, I doubt anything has changed in the last half century, at least not for the better."

"The pictures make Fairlawn look like a great place."

Angela wasn't going to give up. John took another tack. "Are you running a fever?"

There was a second of silence as she absorbed the apparent non sequitur. "No. Why would you think that?"

"It's the only reason I can imagine for this discussion." John softened his words by adding, "You're a terrific realtor with an almost uncanny nose for bargains, but you're way off base on this one." He looked at the before-and-after pictures that lined his office. "You know that my expertise is in urban areas, not a has-been mill town in the middle of nowhere."

"Let me guess. Was that a subtle way of telling me you're not interested in this incredible estate?"

John nodded. "You've got that right."

That had been yesterday. So why was he in the car now, less than twenty-four hours later, heading for that very same has-been mill town in the middle of nowhere? John turned up the stereo, hoping that the sound of his favorite Beethoven sonata would provide an answer. Admittedly, it was a beautiful spring day, an ideal time to take the Ferrari for a spin. But that was no reason to have canceled his tennis match with Rick. It wasn't as if he wanted to see his grandparents' home. It wasn't as if Angela's description had intrigued him. Of course it wasn't. Perhaps he was the one who was running a fever. That was the only reason John could find for this totally irrational act.

He flicked on the turn signal and exited the interstate. According to the map, Hidden Falls was twenty miles off the highway, connected to civilization by a small gray line that John hoped was a paved road. When county road 307 turned into Forest Street just after the peeling WELCOME TO HIDDEN

FALLS sign, he braked. It wasn't simply that he didn't want an overzealous officer who had never seen a red Ferrari suggesting that he was exceeding the speed limit. John also wanted to see if the town was as hopeless as he'd expected.

It was worse. The sole signs of commerce were an anemic strip mall that had been enclosed in an attempt to encourage shoppers to linger, a theater that boasted only two films, and a grocery store hardly larger than a mini-mart. No doubt about it, Granddad was right to leave. There was no future here. *So, why on earth had he come?* John shook his head, unable to articulate a single reason. Still, as long as he was here, he might as well see what Angela called the ancestral estate.

He turned onto Bridge Street, driving well below the posted speed limit. The park that Granddad had mentioned was still there, across the street from the now vacant train station, but there was no sign of the carousel that Grandma had claimed was the town's pride and joy. As John crossed the river, he noted that the iron bridge had been replaced sometime in the last couple decades, although as he turned onto River Road, he wasn't sure why. Granddad had spoken of the three large houses that graced this side of the river, and how the families there were considered Hidden Falls' aristocracy. It appeared that only one remained, and that one, Angela had told him, was vacant.

It was ridiculous to have come all this way. He should have met Rick for their weekly tennis match, then gone back to the office. Heaven knows there was enough work to keep him busy seven days a week. And yet, here he was, the powerful car slowed to little more than a crawl as he approached the house that had been home to six generations of Morelands.

John pulled into the driveway, trying not to shudder at the deep ruts and the damage they might inflict on the Ferrari's undercarriage, as he rounded the final bend. *Oh!* Instinctively, John's foot hit the brake. The car skidded to a stop as he tried to catch his breath. Who would have thought, who could have dreamt that the sight of Fairlawn would hit him like a blow to the solar plexus? He'd seen pictures; he'd heard stories, but nothing had prepared him for this visceral reaction to his family's former home.

It was nothing more than bricks and mortar, John told himself. Bricks and mortar that needed work. Lots of work. Shrubs blocked the front windows; the lawn had gone to weeds; the brick would have to be repointed; the slate roof needed replacing. The logical half of John's brain registered those details while he tried to return his heart to its normal pace. Why was it—how could it be—that he felt as if he'd somehow come home? What an absurd thought! Home was a perfectly appointed condo with a view of the Manhattan skyline. Home was definitely not a rose brick building whose towers and crenellations made it look like a robber baron's idea of a European castle.

He needed to leave. Instead, John found himself parking the car and climbing out, almost running as he circled the house, eager to see it from every angle. When he'd completed the first circuit, his feet slowed, and he started around it again. This time he studied the building, peering into a few windows as he tried to understand the floor plan. *Was that the ballroom where one of his ancestors had been married? Did the darkened brick mean that this was the wing that had been the site of the tragic fire?* John shook his head in disgust. It didn't matter. There was no reason to be here and even less to be speculating on the interior of a building that he had no intention of entering. It was time to return home.

His stomach growled, reminding him that he'd had only a sketchy breakfast and no lunch. *All right,* he muttered to himself. Even though it was not a bustling metropolis, there had to be some place that served food in Hidden Falls. He retraced his way across the river, then continued north on Bridge Street. Judging from the old buildings, this had once been the center of town. What had formerly been commercial establishments appeared to have been converted—poorly, he might add—into low rent apartments. He would have taken a different approach. John shook his head again. There was no point in speculating about ways to renovate this town. He was going to have a burger and fries—surely the golden arches had made it here—and then find the quickest way back to New Jersey.

Spotting a shiny silver-colored building one block over, he turned toward the diner. Perhaps luck would be with him and the food would be edible. John parked directly in front of the main window and requested a booth next to that window. Though this did not appear to be a high crime area, there was no sense in taking chances with the Ferrari.

To his relief, the diner was clean and the menu, while not extensive, featured the comfort food that he'd expected. His order of a burger and fries might not have elicited any comments, but it was clear that his presence did. John heard the murmurs from the booth behind him and the loud, but indistinguishable commentary in the kitchen. Strangers, it appeared, were not common in Hidden Falls, especially strangers driving expensive red Italian sports cars.

In less time than he'd thought possible, the waitress slid a plate of food in front of him. "Enjoy!" she said with a perky smile.

John nodded and took a bite of the burger. To his surprise, it was cooked to perfection, as flavorful as any he'd ever tasted, and the fries were crisp without being greasy. At least one thing in this town wasn't hopeless.

As he savored the simple meal, John heard the front door open and the bell tinkle, announcing a new patron's arrival.

Patrons, he corrected himself at the sound of two voices. Women. Fairly young. He made the assessment quickly, confirming it as the women passed him. They were both clad in jeans and wool jackets, but the similarities ended there. One was tall, with the dark brown hair, deep blue eyes, and pale complexion that he'd discovered was common in Ireland, while the other was an all-American beauty with light brown hair, creamy skin, and light eyes. She'd have drawn any man's eye, if she hadn't been with her friend. As it was, the brunet's vibrant looks eclipsed everyone in the diner. She was beauty pageant gorgeous, not that John would wish that fate on anyone. He'd grown up with too many stories of what happened to contestants once the lights faded.

When the waitress seated the women three booths away, the beautiful brunet took the bench that faced him. She kept her eyes focused on her friend, glancing at John only once. That was enough. He'd seen the faint amusement in her eyes and the almost scornful look she'd given him. If he hadn't known better, he would have said that she'd noticed his cashmere sweater and the Rolex and found him somehow lacking because of them. That was, of course, ridiculous, almost as ridiculous as the fact that he was in Hidden Falls.

Though he admonished himself not to look at her, John's eyes refused his brain's command, and he noticed the animated way the brunet responded to her friend's comments and the warm smile she gave the waitress. They were not being treated to the beautiful woman's disdain as John was. He didn't care. In a few minutes, he'd be back in the car and Hidden Falls would be nothing more than an unpleasant memory.

John dipped a fry in catsup, chewing slowly as he looked out the window for the twentieth time. The Ferrari was still there, as it had been the previous nineteen times. He blinked. He was looking at a red sports car, parked in front of the diner. He knew that. There was no one in it. He knew that, too. But for a second, he would have sworn that the car was a Model T and that it had pulled up in front of Fairlawn. The front door of the mansion had opened and a woman had stood there, dressed in an evening gown, her slender neck and wrists encircled with diamonds.

John blinked again, then swallowed, trying to dispel the image. He'd never been one for hallucinations or even fanciful daydreams. Why then was he picturing the jeans and sweater-clad woman who had regarded him with such disdain standing at Fairlawn, wearing a costume that was at least a century old?

It was absurd. Totally, completely absurd. And yet . . . As he swallowed his last bite of burger, John's brain began to whirl.

His brain had taken a leave of absence. John frowned at his reflection as he began to shave. An extended leave of absence. That was the only explanation he could find for the fact that, after the worst night he'd spent in years, he was still considering the preposterous idea. Imagine, John Moreland, the man who'd made his fortune gentrifying urban areas, renovating one single building in an almost rural location and turning it into—his frown deepened—a luxury hotel. You'd think that a night spent on a lumpy mattress, his sleep further disturbed by the incessant sound of trucks revving their engines to climb the hill would have dissuaded him. It hadn't. Instead, he'd wakened more invigorated than he'd been in weeks.

He toweled his face, then reached for his cell phone, thankful that he didn't have a video phone. He didn't want anyone he knew seeing him looking like this. What had possessed him to pull into the Wal-Mart parking lot last night and buy generic jeans, sneakers, and a sweatshirt in addition to the basic toiletries? Surely it wasn't the memory of the beautiful brunet's amusement at his city clothes.

Angela listened in silence when he asked her to contact the listing realtor and arrange for a tour of Fairlawn.

"I won't say 'I told you so.'" Though she managed to keep her voice steady, John heard the hint of mirth. He couldn't blame her.

"You'd better not, or I'll invite someone else to the art show," he teased.

"You wouldn't."

"Of course I wouldn't. It wouldn't be any fun without your commentary." Angela had been a Fine Arts student, and her knowledge of the field made her an entertaining companion at the various art events John felt obliged to attend.

"I'm glad you appreciate me." This time there was no doubt that Angela was laughing. "Let me call the local agent and set up your appointment."

"I need an hour to get there." There had been no hotels in Hidden Falls and, to John's dismay, a major convention had filled all the reputable ones in Binghamton, leaving him with what he was now calling Motel Lumpy.

Angela chuckled. "John, this isn't Manhattan you're dealing with. People move slower in the 'burbs. It'll take longer than an hour."

The 'burbs. If only Hidden Falls could be dignified with that appellation. When he entered the town for the second time in less than twenty-four hours, John turned off Forest, hoping that one of the parallel streets would be more impressive. It wasn't. Main Street, despite its name, appeared to have no commercial establishments, and the older houses that lined the road could benefit from a coat of paint. Of course, it wasn't the town that had intrigued him, but the house on the hill.

John took a deep breath, exhaling slowly. Perhaps the

strange attraction that he'd felt had been a product of his imagination, the result of skipping lunch. Hadn't he read that people hallucinated when they were starving? Not that he'd been starving, of course, but there had to be an explanation, a rational one, for the way he'd reacted to that pile of bricks. When he saw it this morning, he'd feel differently. It would be nothing more than an old building. The magic would be gone.

It wasn't. As he approached Fairlawn, John felt the same inexplicable pull that had bothered him the previous afternoon. It was almost as if the house were welcoming him, inviting him to enter it. Absurd. Totally absurd. Just as absurd as picturing the brunet in the doorway.

He parked the car, then walked slowly, trying to envision the changes he'd make. The first thing he needed to do was find a way to keep his guests separated from the town. It wasn't simply that they'd be appalled by the shabby buildings and lack of basic amenities, but—judging from the reaction that his own appearance had caused—they'd be regarded with suspicion by the townspeople if they ventured outside the hotel's grounds. Word would spread, and Fairlawn would be doomed.

John paced, his even strides measuring the lawn. Good. The space to the southwest was large enough for a helicopter pad. He made a quick decision. Room rates would include transportation from major cities. He'd market it as yet another upscale service, sparing his guests the hassles of traffic. Once they arrived, Fairlawn would be self-contained. He'd turn it into one of those "destination resorts" where every possible need was met. There would be so much to do here that there'd be no reason for anyone to leave the premises and see the depressed—and depressing—downtown of Hidden Falls. *It was,* he said to himself, *an excellent plan.*

As he walked around the building, John studied the exterior. Though the brick needed work, nothing indicated major problems. That was good. So, too, was the presence of an outbuilding that Angela claimed had once held a small carousel factory. It appeared large enough to be converted into accommodations for the staff. Another plus. If the resort were to succeed, it would need highly trained staff, probably lured from other luxury hotels. They'd be no more willing to live in Hidden Falls than John himself.

Angela had told him that the house had an unusually deep cellar. Assuming that there were no structural problems, it could be used for the spa that would be Fairlawn's major attraction. It might even be possible to create an indoor lap pool there, although John would have to see the area to be certain. He smiled. Though the town was beyond dismal, Fairlawn had potential.

He was still smiling when he rounded the corner of the south wing. As he recalled, there was a small garden there. During the summer, it could be the source of fresh vegetables—another draw for the moneyed crowd. John started humming softly. Perhaps this wasn't such a crazy idea, after all.

And then he saw her. Though she was bent over one of the flower beds, the way his pulse began to race as if he'd injected caffeine directly into his bloodstream, told him this was no stranger. For whatever reason, the beautiful brunet from the diner was here at Fairlawn, puttering around in the garden.

She wasn't the owner; Angela had said that the current owner was someone from out of town. So why was she here, and why did the mere sight of her make John feel as if he were a teenager again? It had been years since a woman had elevated his heart rate more than a game of tennis. This was not a feeling he welcomed.

"Do you make a habit of trespassing?" The instant the

words were out of his mouth, John regretted them. While it was true that he didn't want her disturbing his exploration, there was no reason to be rude.

She straightened and stared at him, one eyebrow raised ever so slightly. John took a deep breath. She was even more beautiful than he remembered. Today her hair was pulled back in a ponytail, partially hidden by an ancient ball cap, and the sweat suit she wore was frayed around the edges. Despite the unsophisticated clothing, the look she gave him was regal.

"I could say the same to you." Her voice was cool, but the way those deep blue eyes moved slowly from John's face down to his sneaker-clad feet left no doubt that she was amused by his newly acquired wardrobe.

"Actually," he said, drawing out the word, "I'm not trespassing." Though there was no reason to explain, he did. "I have an appointment."

The brunet's eyebrow rose another half inch, her skepticism apparent. "To do what?"

This was ridiculous. She was the intruder, not he. She was the one who should be answering questions, not he. He owed her no explanations, and yet John found himself saying, "To see the house. There is a For Sale sign in front."

She shrugged. "It's been there so long that I don't notice it anymore."

John raised one of his brows, wondering whether she was being deliberately evasive or whether she'd forgotten his original question. In either case, the result was that she still hadn't explained why she was picking Fairlawn's flowers. "Do you always work in someone else's garden?" She probably lived in an apartment and had no green space of her own.

"Actually," she said, her tone mocking his use of the word, "this is a rare variety of daffodils." She gestured toward the flowers that she'd cut and laid on the ground. "It seemed a shame to let them bloom here where no one can enjoy them."

"I see." What John saw was that the beautiful stranger was distracting him. Wouldn't Angela laugh if she could see him now, discussing daffodils when he ought to be planning his negotiating strategy? John felt like a gyroscope that had suddenly lost its equilibrium, and the reason wasn't hard to find. She had to go. The tall brunet in worn clothing and muddy gardening gloves had to leave before the realtor arrived. John Moreland, CEO of JBM Enterprises, needed all his wits about him to negotiate. He couldn't do that with her nearby, disturbing him with that smile and the faint scent of perfume.

"I won't tell the owner that you've taken flowers if you leave now."

This time she laughed, "How very kind of you, Mr. . . ."

"Baxter. John Baxter." It was one of the names he used when buying property. "And you're . . ."

"Leaving."

Chapter Two

"Thank you, my dear. The daffodils are handsome."

Handsome? Claire took a deep breath, trying to slow her pulse as she trimmed the last flower stem. What was handsome was the stranger, the man named John Baxter, the same man who was making her heart beat so erratically. Hidden Falls had never seen anyone like him. *Be honest, Claire,* she admonished herself. *You've never seen anyone like him, either.* Tall, dark, and handsome was a cliché. Fortunately, since Claire abhorred clichés, John Baxter did not fit that one. He was tall, *blond*, handsome, and obviously out of his element here. And that, she had to admit, was part of his appeal. It had been amusing to watch a man whose whole being shrieked "urban" try to be inconspicuous at the diner. Even today's obviously new, obviously cheap clothes had done nothing to dispel the aura of power and privilege that clung to him like bark to a tree.

"No one arranges flowers as well as you do." Dimly Claire was aware of her grandmother's words. "But I think I'd prefer that you use the bleach jug instead of this Waterford vase."

Claire blinked and turned toward Glinda. "What kind of nonsense is that?" The woman was sitting at the kitchen table, her eyes narrowing as she stared at her.

"It's as I thought." Glinda's smile could only be described as triumphant. "You weren't listening to me when I told you how fortunate it was that you majored in Home Economics, or whatever it is they call it these days."

"It's FCS, Family and Consumer Science," Claire said, addressing the easy part of Glinda's observation. "Sorry. I'm a little preoccupied this morning."

Glinda muttered something that sounded like "More than a little," then raised her voice to say, "Judging from that faraway expression, the reason for your preoccupation was a man. Hallelujah!"

Claire wouldn't give her grandmother the satisfaction of admitting she was right. "I have more important things to worry about than a man," she informed Glinda as she set the flower vase on the table. "First on the list is the school's future."

"The school wouldn't put a sparkle in your eyes." Glinda smiled again. "You can deny it all you want, Claire Conners, but you've met a man, and not a minute too soon. Don't you see? If the school closes, you can marry him and stay home and . . ."

"Raise your great-grandbabies." Claire finished the sentence, knowing there was only one conclusion that would satisfy Glinda. "We've been through this before." About a million times, give or take one or two. "My answer hasn't changed. I'm not looking for a man; I'm not planning to marry; and you'll just have to wait for those great-grandchildren."

Glinda smiled. "Definitely a man."

A man who was an enigma. Claire couldn't help wondering why someone who drove a Ferrari and wore clothes that cost as much as the annual income of the average Hidden Falls family was considering moving here. Even today's cheap chic attire couldn't disguise the fact that he was born with a silver—make that a gold—spoon in his mouth. There were none of those in Hidden Falls. Though it had once been home to a few very wealthy families, the Morelands foremost among them, those days were long past.

Claire glanced at her wristwatch. "I've gotta run," she said. "Literally." It was time to meet Ruby for their weekly jog. Not that she needed the exercise today. Claire had walked up the hill to Fairlawn, donning her oldest clothes for the trip, because she'd known she'd be kneeling on muddy ground. That was why John Baxter had seen her at less than her best. Not that it mattered. As she'd told Glinda, Claire was not looking for a husband.

They were doing leg stretches when Ruby said, "I started my job search last night. I sent off a bunch of e-mails to my sorority sisters and everyone I met at conferences, asking if they knew of openings for math teachers." Ruby straightened, then shook her head in mock dismay. "I knew there had to be a reason I kept all those business cards."

Claire laughed. "You kept them because you're compulsively organized."

"I suppose that's better than being called a pack rat, which is my brother's favorite term. Seriously, Claire, it's not too early to begin looking for a new position."

They started running, matching their strides with the ease of long-term jogging partners, despite the difference in their heights. "I don't disagree with you," Claire admitted, "but let's be honest. You're in a better situation. The new school will need math teachers, but FCS is a luxury. Kids can graduate without it, so when there's a budget crunch, it's one of the first departments to be eliminated."

Ruby grimaced. "Gerry didn't say anything about budget problems."

"But money is the reason for consolidating schools. Even

if they keep FCS, there are teachers at Rockledge and Bartonsville with more seniority." Claire had considered her prospects, and they weren't good. "At any rate, I'm not holding my breath for an offer of a position. Now, can we change the subject? I don't want to spend a nice day like this thinking about unemployment."

"Okay." As they rounded the corner, Ruby shot a grin at Claire. "I was at Link's this morning," she said, referring to the town's sole grocery store.

"Another donut run? I thought you'd sworn off them." Though it mystified Claire and the rest of Ruby's friends how she could eat high fat foods and gain no weight, one of Ruby's New Year's resolutions had been to eliminate junk food.

"Times of stress require strong medicine."

"Since when are jelly donuts medicine?"

"Since I declared them the foundation of the food pyramid." With another mocking grin, Ruby continued. "Keep this up, Ms. Healthy Eater, and I won't tell you what I discovered." They jogged in place, waiting for the Hidden Falls equivalent of rush traffic—two cars—to pass before they crossed the street.

"A fate worse than death!" Ruby had an uncanny knack for ferreting out information. "My lips are sealed." Claire imitated her students, her fingers pretending to lock her lips. "No more nutritional advice. So, what did you hear?"

"You know our mysterious stranger, the one we saw in the diner."

Indeed she did. Not only was he the only stranger—mysterious or otherwise—to enter Hidden Falls in the last month, but he was the only one whose behavior had verged on rudeness. The fact that he'd dismissed her as if she were an errant child, practically ordering her off Fairlawn, was the sole reason she continued to think about him. Of course it was. "John Baxter," Claire said.

Ruby shot her a quick glance as she increased the pace. "Who are you talking about? His name is John Moreland."

For the first time, Claire's step faltered. "*The* John Moreland?" If that was true, it was no wonder he appeared to have more money than anyone could need.

Ruby nodded. "John Moreland, as in urban renovation, megabucks, and a descendent of the first owner of Fairlawn. Rumor has it he wants to buy the old place."

"The rumor's right. I saw him there, waiting for the realtor." But why had he given her a false name when it was obvious others knew his true identity? Perhaps the man was eccentric as well as being rich as Croesus.

"I wonder what he's planning to do with Fairlawn."

Claire shrugged. "I can't even begin to guess." She had been mystified about why a man whose appearance shrieked "affluent urban" was considering living at Fairlawn. Now that she knew John Baxter was really John Moreland, it made even less sense, unless Fairlawn was only the first piece of a plan. Maybe he had plans for all of Hidden Falls. The man Claire had met didn't appear to be one who'd move back here for sentimental reasons.

"It could be good for the town. If he renovates Fairlawn—which the poor old place needs—it'll mean more jobs, at least during construction."

"Are you thinking one project would bring more residents?" Ruby's tone told Claire she knew how unlikely that was.

"Maybe it'll be more than one. A girl can dream, can't she?"

John plugged in his headset, knowing this would be a long call. He'd waited until he'd arrived home before making it, because he wanted to be able to take notes. "I like it," he told Angela. "The interior is in better shape than I'd expected." The cellar, as he had hoped, was deep enough that he could locate the spa there, and there were no obvious structural deficiencies. Those were facts. His realtor needed to know them, as did his architect. What they didn't need to know was the totally irrational reaction he had had to the old house, how much he had enjoyed walking through Fairlawn, and how each step had made him more certain that buying the building was the right move.

Though years of neglect had taken their toll, Fairlawn was ideally suited for the kind of luxury hotel that John had envisioned the night before. The common rooms on the main floor were spacious, and the discovery of what the listing realtor called the "morning room" had been a pleasant surprise. Though not large, it could be turned into a meeting room, which would extend the potential client base from couples looking for relaxation and pampering to corporations seeking locations for critical off-site meetings and planning sessions. Even the servants' quarters on the top floor had more possibilities than he'd expected. Though they would be smaller than the bedrooms on the second floor, the pitched ceilings in the servants' rooms suggested a more casual décor that would appeal to some guests, as would the more affordable price he would charge for them.

"I want to buy it," John said firmly. "What do you think is the lowest bid they'll accept?" He leaned back in his chair, admiring the reflection of the setting sun on Manhattan's skyscrapers.

If Angela was surprised by John's decision, she wisely said nothing. "It's going to be more expensive than yesterday. Our cover's blown. Someone figured out that you're John Moreland, not John Baxter."

That was annoying but not a showstopper. "All right. Since there's no point in denying the obvious, let's play on the Moreland name. Present me as the prodigal son who's returning to town. If we act as if I want to make this my weekend residence, we may get a lower price than if they know it's going to be commercial."

Half an hour later, when they'd finished discussing pricing scenarios, Angela said, "You'll probably need a zoning variance for the hotel." She paused for effect, then added, "If there's such a thing as zoning in The-Middle-of-Nowhere, New York."

The sun had set. Now the city sparkled with neon and fluorescent lights. It was a far cry from Hidden Falls, The-Middle-of-Nowhere, New York. "I'll worry about that after the sale is complete." Though part of John's past success was based on addressing all concerns, including zoning, before making an offer, this was different. Even if there were restrictions, he couldn't imagine he would have a problem obtaining a variance. A town as badly on the skids as Hidden Falls wouldn't turn down anything that was likely to generate revenue or increase the tax base.

"Great. I'll have the paperwork ready for your signature tomorrow." Angela paused for a second. "You will be home tomorrow, won't you?"

"You bet. There's no reason to go back to Hidden Falls."

But less than two weeks later, John was returning, this time as the new owner of Fairlawn. It seemed that everyone was happy. The previous owner had been so delighted to unload the property that John had gotten a good price, even using his own name. John was happy about that. So was Angela, although she claimed that her pleasure was more than financial. When they'd met to celebrate, she told John that her commission was only part of the appeal of this particular deal. Now that her part was complete, she was looking forward to attending the first costume ball.

Though it had been a fanciful thought, John had been unable to dismiss the image he'd had of the brunet—Ms. Leaving, as he now called her—in historic clothing, and he'd realized that occasional costume balls would be another way to increase occupancy at Fairlawn. Women enjoyed the chance to return to a former era, if only for an evening, and while the men were likely to be less enthusiastic, John knew they'd agree.

Even John's architect and best friend Rick was happy. Though Rick had been surprised when John had told him about his plans, surprise had turned into enthusiasm for the new project, and he'd agreed that he would once again provide all the architectural consulting John needed.

Everything was set, with one exception. It had been Rick who'd raised the question of lodging during construction, asking whether there would be enough room for himself and his son, or whether he should plan his visits as day trips. Normally, John maintained a pied à terre at his work sites, and normally it was large enough for Rick and Josh.

As Rick had reminded him, John needed a living space near this job site, and it most definitely would not be Motel Lumpy. That was the reason he was now approaching the outskirts of Hidden Falls. It had nothing—nothing at all—to do with the fact that he might see Ms. Leaving again. A woman—any woman—was a complication John didn't need. And if he were looking for complications, it certainly would not be one who regarded him as if he were an exhibit at the zoo.

"Good afternoon, Mr. Moreland."

John wasn't surprised when the waitress at the diner greeted him by name. Rumors spread quickly, particularly in a small town. He'd counted on that, as well as the fact that diners served more than food. "Good afternoon, Miss . . ." He let his voice trail off. Unlike wait staff in a larger city, she wore no name tag. Since it was likely that everyone in Hidden Falls knew each other, there was no need.

"Betsy. Just Betsy," she said. "What can I get for you?"

"A turkey club sandwich; fries; coffee, black; and some information."

Betsy, just Betsy, blinked as she reached for the coffee pot. "What kind of information?"

"I need a place to stay while the men are working on Fairlawn, and I didn't see a hotel." Nor had his Google search revealed any form of accommodation, not even a rooming house.

"There aren't any," Betsy confirmed. "Hidden Falls doesn't attract many visitors."

John suspected that was an understatement. "Is there no place closer than Binghamton?" That was an hour away. It was odd. Though he routinely spent as much time commuting from his office into Manhattan for meetings, he didn't relish the idea of an hour's drive here.

Betsy was silent for a moment, obviously trying to be helpful. "If you're not real fussy," she said at last, "you might try Mrs. Conners. She's got a spare room." When John nodded, Betsy continued. "Her place is on Maple just past Moreland. You can't miss it. It's the only yellow house in town."

"Thanks." While he wouldn't use the word "fussy," John had to admit that he was decidedly particular about lodging. What was he getting himself into?

"No, Chuck," Claire said when she saw the teenager preparing to slide the ramekins into the oven. "You can't make crème brulée without a *bain marie*. Your custard will curdle."

"Oh, Chuck, you dummy. Everyone knows that." Jackie, who along with Chuck, was charged with making dessert for the after-school cooking club, didn't bother to hide her sarcasm as she started to boil a kettle of water. When poured around the ramekins, the hot water would form the water bath or *bain marie* that ensured a perfect texture for the classic dessert.

"Sure everyone knows that," Chuck said, "just like everyone knows how to hold the torch." He gestured toward Jackie's singed eyebrows, the result of last week's attempt to make crème brulée. "Everyone except you."

"If you two can't play well together," Claire said, her tone as light as she could make it, "I'll have to take your toys away." Laughter greeted her threat. "Including the thermometer." The instant read thermometer was a recent addition to the school's kitchen and the one utensil that every one of the Gourmet Wannabes had agreed was essential.

"Okay. Okay." The two teenagers raised their hands in surrender. "We'll be good."

And they would. Claire knew that, just as she knew that the reason for the uncharacteristic bickering was that the students had heard rumors about the school's closing. In a town as small as Hidden Falls, there were few secrets. Though the kids had said nothing to her, they were unable to hide the fact that they were worried. So was she.

The truth was, she enjoyed teaching. Even if it wasn't the career she'd once dreamt of, Claire found it satisfying— surprisingly so. Unlike Ruby, whose math courses were required for graduation, the FCS subjects Claire taught were electives. That meant that, while she had fewer students than Ruby, Claire's pupils were there by choice, not because the State of New York mandated it. They were normally eager to learn, which made Claire's job easier. Her students' curiosity kept her on her toes, and serving as faculty advisor for the Gourmet Wannabes was the proverbial icing on the cake. It was a good job, a rewarding one, and that made it painful to realize that it might end.

"Excellent, Annie," Claire said, tasting a spoonful of sauce. "Your coq au vin is just right." Unfortunately, not much else was.

An hour and a half later, Claire turned the corner onto

Maple Street. Except in the worst of weather, she preferred to walk to work. The exercise, she told Glinda, helped her unwind at the end of the day and gave her a chance to think. These days, however, Claire would have preferred less time for introspection.

Her pace increased slightly as she approached the house that had been her home for as long as she could remember. Though she had pictures, she had no recollection of the apartment where she'd lived during the year and a half that her parents had believed they could juggle parenthood with careers. No one had taken her back to see her first home. Why would they, when it marked the sole failure in Ken and Susan Conners' lives? This was home, and Glinda was her parent. Claire wouldn't think about the alternative, any more than she would think about the school's future. Instead . . . Her eyes widened as she saw the unfamiliar car parked in the drive. Nondescript gray sedan, New Jersey plates, possibly a rental. She felt a surge of adrenaline. Had Mom and Dad come for a visit? Claire shook her head. They never made unscheduled trips to Hidden Falls. So, whose car was it?

"I'm home, Glinda," Claire called as she slid her coat onto a wooden hanger.

"Come in here, dear." Judging from the sound of her voice, Glinda was in what she persisted in calling the parlor. "I have a surprise for you."

Claire tried not to wince. The last surprise had been a set of knives her grandmother had purchased from an itinerant salesman. Though the intricately carved wooden handles were a work of art, the blades were so dull that they could almost pass airport security.

After the tension at school and the momentary burst of adrenaline, Claire wasn't certain she was ready for another surprise. Still, there was no point in delaying the inevitable.

Her heels clicked on the hardwood floor as she approached the front of the house. Although Glinda continued to chatter, her visitor was silent, giving Claire no clue to his or her identity. She entered the room and stopped short. Glinda was right. This was a surprise. Seated on the chintz sofa, somehow looking as if he belonged there, was the man who had called himself John Baxter.

Claire raised an eyebrow in what she hoped was a look of cool contempt. At least today they were on her turf. At least today she was wearing professional clothing, a charcoal gray skirt, lighter gray blazer, and a sapphire blouse, instead of grungy sweats.

John rose, inclining his head in what could be construed as a greeting. Though it had been fleeting, Claire had caught the surprise in his eyes. Whatever had brought him here, he hadn't expected to see her. Of course not. A man like that didn't pay visits to small town schoolteachers.

"I was going to introduce you," Glinda said, her eyes darting from John to Claire and back again, "but it appears that you've already met."

Under false pretenses. Rather than voice her thoughts and upset her grandmother, Claire said as mildly as she could, "Introductions might be in order."

"Well, then." Glinda gave Claire a piercing look, as if to warn her that she was in store for another round of inquisition once John Moreland left. "Claire, this is John Moreland."

"Not John Baxter?" She couldn't resist the question. Though he drove a less flamboyant car today, John Whatever-His-Last-Name was wearing another of what Claire was beginning to consider his trademark cashmere sweaters and finely tailored slacks. Loafers that looked as if they'd been custom made for him completed the ensemble and left no doubt that the man beneath the clothing had more than his share of earthly goods.

The man in question smiled. "Actually," he said, emphasizing the word as he had when they'd met in the garden, "my full name is John Baxter Moreland."

"So you didn't lie, at least not completely. I'm glad to hear that." It was a crime of omission, not commission. In Claire's book, that was better, but only marginally.

Obviously surprised by the sarcasm, Glinda leaned toward John, her expression warm and welcoming. "This is my granddaughter, Claire Conners."

"Not Ms. Leaving?" he asked, his tone a duplicate of Claire's.

Touché. Claire nodded slightly, acknowledging the fact that she had exhibited her share of rudeness by not giving him her name. That had been uncharacteristically petty of her. All right. The score was even, but that didn't explain why John Baxter Moreland was in her home.

"Ms. Leaving? I assume that that's a private joke." A satisfied smile crossed Glinda's face as she settled back into her chair. She waited until both Claire and John were seated before she said, "I have the best news." Her smile was more brilliant than normal, her eyes sparkling with obvious delight. "My dear, John is going to rent your old bedroom suite when he's in town. I promised him meals, too."

Over my dead body! Claire bit back her instinctive reaction. It would be petty to object to Glinda's plan, and Claire refused to be petty. Not again. Still, she felt as if she'd been punched in the stomach and all the breath forced out of her. This was a surprise, all right. An unpleasant one.

"I see." Though she had had no regrets when she'd moved down a floor to be closer to Glinda, Claire didn't like the idea of anyone—especially John Baxter Moreland—using the rooms she'd spent so much time decorating. They were all she had left of her dream.

"If the meals are too much trouble," John said, appearing

to sense Claire's distress but not knowing the reason for it, "I can eat at the diner."

"Nonsense." Glinda gave Claire no time to reply. "Claire is an excellent cook. She needs someone besides me to appreciate her skills."

Great, Glinda. Why don't you just hang an "available for marriage" sign around my neck? Though it took what felt like a super human effort, Claire kept a smile on her face. "I hope my grandmother explained that this establishment is modified American plan." Though she didn't like the idea of having a live-in guest, it wouldn't be difficult to increase the servings of breakfast and dinner; however, she had no intention of providing lunch.

"She did, and I assure you, Ms. Conners . . ."

"Claire." Glinda interjected the word.

"Claire." He nodded, but Claire noticed that no smile accompanied the nod. "I'll try not to be a burden."

It wasn't his fault, she reflected. The man needed a place to stay while Fairlawn was under construction. If she was going to be annoyed with anyone, it should be Glinda, who had clearly seen John Moreland's arrival as an opportunity to matchmake. But how could she be angry with Glinda? It wasn't as if she'd ever told her grandmother how special the attic suite was to her. Quite the contrary. When Glinda had fallen and broken her ankle, Claire had claimed that she was tired of the extra flight of stairs. She had never told her grandmother that the only reason she'd given up her suite was to care for her. Glinda wouldn't have allowed that.

"I'm glad you're renovating Fairlawn," Claire said honestly. "The town needs someone with your . . ." She paused for an instant to glare at Glinda. ". . . skills. Our downtown area, as I'm sure you've noticed, would benefit from an infusion of—what did *The New York Times* call it?—'carefully planned and perfectly executed urban gentrification.' "

When it had seemed definite that John Moreland would become an occasional resident of Hidden Falls, Claire had done her homework, checking all the online references she could find and reviewing the library's Hidden Falls history section. Though John had, to Claire's knowledge, never visited the town until two weeks before, the librarian had granted him honorary citizenship simply because of his name.

Claire could now recite the basic facts of John's life: how his mother had been a Miss America contestant, how his father was a highly successful trial attorney reputed to be the power behind the scenes for several prominent politicians, how their marriage had ended in divorce, and how the senior Mr. Moreland had remarried not once but twice. More than half the file had been devoted to John himself, recording high school sports awards, college graduation, and even pictures of him attending cultural events, as well as articles praising his work and a video of him accepting an award. The man was the closest Hidden Falls had to a living legend.

The faint smile that had crossed the living legend's face disappeared. "My focus is on Fairlawn."

Claire nodded. She might not like the fact that he would be boarding here, but she did like the improvements he could make to her hometown. "As it should be. That will give you a place to live during the next phases of the project." The sooner Fairlawn was habitable, the sooner she would have her house back to normal. And, once the all too disturbing John Moreland was gone, she would be able to enjoy watching the downtown take shape.

"My commitment is to Fairlawn." John shifted his feet ever so slightly. If Claire hadn't known better, she would have said that he was uncomfortable with the discussion. Why would he be? Did he think anyone would demand exorbitant prices for the vacant stores and the dilapidated mill if they knew he was interested in acquiring them? The current owners were out-of-town investors who would undoubtedly be thrilled to unload property that had failed to provide any income.

Claire didn't have to close her eyes to imagine the downtown area restored and once more bustling with activity. New stores, new businesses, new residents. John Moreland might not be a miracle worker, but he was the best chance Hidden Falls had.

Chapter Three

"Claire dear, why don't you give John a tour of the town?" Glinda's smile was deceptively innocent as she added, "I've warned him that tonight's dinner will be simple, so you don't have to worry about that."

Claire returned the smile. While there was no doubt that Glinda still had a matchmaking gleam in her eyes and that this was a ploy to ensure that Claire and John spent time together, there was nothing Claire could do to stop it without resorting to rudeness. She wouldn't be rude to the man who had it in his power to save Hidden Falls.

"I don't claim to be the Chamber of Commerce," she told John, "but I'd be glad to show you around." At least Glinda wouldn't be with them, praising Claire's domestic skills. A slow flush rose to Claire's cheeks as she considered what Glinda might have told John before she arrived home. The woman was determined to see Claire married, and soon.

"Thanks." Clearly more at ease than Claire, John rose. "Your car or mine?"

"You'll see more if I drive." Claire led the way through

the kitchen, where she grabbed her bag and keys. If John noticed the blue-and-white gingham and the *Wizard of Oz* posters on the walls, he said nothing. Men, at least in Claire's experience, were less attuned to décor than she. Of course, most men didn't have her background.

When she reached the garage door, she turned toward John. "What happened to your fancy car?" she asked, remembering the plain gray sedan parked in front of her house. It was the antithesis of the low-slung red vehicle that had provoked so much discussion at school. Every teenage boy and at least half the girls had wanted to drive that one. Though the Ferrari had been in Hidden Falls for perhaps a grand total of four hours, it seemed that everyone in town had seen it.

John's glance at the sedan reminded Claire of the time in the diner when he'd checked his car more often than a brand new mother did her baby. He definitely cared about his cars. "This is the one I normally use at job sites," he said. "It's more practical."

"Because it attracts less attention?"

He shrugged. "That's a bonus. The fact is, there's an amazing amount of stuff to cart around for one of these projects, everything from blueprints to roofing and tile samples. It's handy to have a trunk for that. And the Ferrari isn't very practical when more than one client needs to be driven somewhere."

Claire climbed behind the wheel of her own vehicle, a dark blue SUV that had transported half a dozen students to a culinary arts fair the day the school bus's water pump had refused to function. Like John's sedan, it was practical, if a bit lacking on the excitement scale.

"I imagine you miss your arrest-me-red sports car."

John fastened his seat belt, then shifted his weight so that he was facing Claire. "I'll have you know that I've never gotten a speeding ticket."

"I notice you didn't claim that you were never stopped."

He laughed. "Did anyone ever tell you that you were too clever? You weren't supposed to notice how carefully I worded that."

What she really wasn't supposed to notice was how laughter softened John Moreland's face. He was a handsome man, no doubt about it, but when he laughed, the sparkle in this eyes and the surprising dimple in his left cheek literally took Claire's breath away. "I suppose you used the Moreland name to talk your way out of a ticket." Thank goodness, her voice sounded normal.

Claire headed south on Maple Street, deciding to take the shortest route to the former center of town. The sooner this trip was over, the better.

"Ouch!" John laid his hand on his chest in mock distress. "That was a direct hit to my ego. I'd prefer to think that my charm convinced the officers that a warning was more than enough punishment."

Claire couldn't help laughing. The man had a sense of humor, and she liked that. He might be out of his element here; she might not like the fact that Glinda had given him her sanctuary, but there was no denying that there was something disarming about him when he laughed. Though the newspaper pictures had shown a strong resemblance between John and his father, it was particularly apparent when they smiled. If Henry Moreland was half as charismatic as his son, it was no wonder he was so successful.

"You look like your father."

Surely it was Claire's imagination that John flinched. "So I've been told." He looked out the window. "This street appears to be all residential."

Claire nodded, recognizing the deliberate change of subject. Whatever the reason, it was clear that John did not want to discuss his father. Fine. It was more important that he see the town.

Though the houses on this stretch of Maple were modest, they were well cared for. That was one of the reasons Claire had chosen this particular street to begin her tour. She knew how critical first impressions were. What she hadn't counted on were the number of people who were outside, apparently gardening or chatting with their neighbors, even though the weather was conducive to neither. The Hidden Falls grapevine must be working overtime to get so many people outdoors so quickly. Claire knew it wasn't her SUV that had provoked the curiosity, but rather its passenger. For the first time, she wished she had heavily tinted windows. At least then John would not be subjected to so many stares. Though he made no comment, he had to be aware of them.

Claire turned onto Main and headed for what used to be the center of town, the corner of Main and Bridge streets. At least here there would be few observers. "At one time there were buildings on all four corners." Claire slowed the car as they approached the intersection. "The hotel and tavern were on this side of Bridge, the bank and church on the other." She gestured toward the white building with the wedding cake steeple. "As you can see, only the church is left." The other three corners were now empty lots, and—unlike the houses on Maple Street—these lots were in need of maintenance. Litter and weeds gave them a desolate air.

As John frowned, Claire wondered if she had made a mistake by pointing out the town's flaws. *Nonsense,* she told herself. *Anyone with even one eye can see what's wrong here. And this man has the ability to change it.*

"The buildings on the left look like post-World War II renovations," he said when they reached the middle of the block. His voice was neutral, as if he were making a casual observation rather than assessing the town's potential for renewal. Surely if he was renovating Fairlawn, he wouldn't stop there. JBM Enterprises' projects were always large in scale. But perhaps this was the way John worked, appraising everything, then deciding how much to include in a project.

Reassured, Claire nodded, confirming John's observation. "The downtown was thriving then, but that was before the advent of big box stores."

"Big boxes?" Something in his tone told Claire John shared Glinda's opinion of the large chain stores. "I didn't notice any of those when I was driving around. Are they further north?"

Claire shook her head. "There were plans for a couple, but they never materialized." Still, by the time it was obvious that the expansion would not occur, the damage had been done. Small shop owners had closed their doors, knowing they could not compete with the chain stores' buying power. That had been the beginning of the end for Hidden Falls' downtown.

As they crossed Rapids Street, John gestured toward the long, two-story buildings that lined both sides of Main. "Those are interesting old buildings. What were they?"

Claire was a little surprised that he didn't know, since the buildings had been part of the Moreland Mills complex. "They were boarding houses for the mill workers." Though the windows were covered with plywood, the detailed brickwork spoke of an earlier era. "I have to admit that I always thought these were more attractive than the new apartment buildings, but they do lack modern conveniences—like indoor plumbing."

Claire slowed the car as John appeared to be studying the boarding houses. "That could be added," he said.

Claire smiled. It was silly to be pleased by his attraction to those particular buildings, and yet when she had learned that

the mysterious stranger was John Moreland, she had hoped
that these old houses would be among the first he'd renovate.

"That's what I thought," she said. "Unfortunately, when
the downtown died, people wanted to live further out, closer
to the schools and stores." But that could be changed, and
with John Moreland at the helm, it would be.

Claire turned right for a block, then took another right
turn. "I imagine you've already seen this," she said as she
stopped the car in front of the five-story red brick building
that dominated the river bank. Claire heard the regret in her
voice as she said, "This used to be the heart of Hidden
Falls." She couldn't explain why she cared about the old
Moreland Mills factory. All she knew was that it had fascinated her for as long as she could remember. When she
would walk by it, she would think about the hundreds of
people who had once worked there, producing some of the
finest textiles in the country. And now it stood vacant, its
windows grimy with years of soot, the clock tower that had
once chimed the start and end of working hours silent.

"I keep thinking that there has to be a way to use it to
bring people downtown again," she said, almost to herself.

"I suppose that's possible."

Claire looked at John, once again surprised by the lack of
enthusiasm in his voice. She would have thought that the
mill would have excited him more than the boarding houses.
Perhaps the coolness was a carefully constructed façade, designed to protect his plans until all the property had been acquired. Claire was not an expert on business negotiations,
but that seemed a likely tactic.

"When I heard your name was Moreland and not Baxter, I
realized how right it was that you were buying Fairlawn."
She put the car into drive and started down the street. "While
I might not use exactly that term, I have friends who would
call it destiny that a Moreland will be the one to renew Hid-

den Falls." John's expression remained impassive, compelling Claire to add, "It was, after all, a Moreland who established the town."

"So my grandfather told me on numerous occasions." John looked to the right, and Claire wondered whether he was deliberately turning his head so that she could not read his expression. "Speaking of grandparents, if it's not prying too much, would you tell me why you live with your grandmother?"

It hadn't been Claire's imagination. Something about their conversation had bothered John enough that he sought an excuse to change the subject, just as he had when she'd mentioned his father.

"Habit, I suppose." Claire continued, knowing that if she didn't tell him the reason for her somewhat unusual living arrangements, Glinda would. "When I was about eighteen months old, my parents realized that juggling a baby and two careers wouldn't work. Like the original Glinda, the Good Witch of the North, she came to the rescue and took me in. I've lived with her ever since, except for college, of course."

John turned, his eyes reflecting his interest. "Now I'm definitely prying, but what kind of careers did your parents have that were more important than their child?"

Though put like that, it sounded cold-blooded, Claire knew the decision had not been an easy one. "One career: flying. They're both pilots." She stopped the car so that she could give John her full attention. "They tried to arrange their schedules so that one of them was home at all times, but it didn't work out." Trying to forestall the normal expressions of sympathy, Claire added, "I was fortunate. Glinda was a wonderful parent."

"She's definitely charismatic."

Claire chuckled, relieved that John seemed to understand that—like his father—her parents were a subject she preferred not to discuss. "That's one way to describe her. Persistent is another. Terriers could take lessons from Glinda."

"I'll keep that in mind."

Increasing her speed as they drove north on Chestnut, Claire slowed again as she approached Ludlow. "You've seen the diner." The silver building stood on the southeastern corner of Chestnut and Ludlow, across from the school complex. Claire made a left turn. "These are the middle and elementary schools," she said, nodding toward the buildings on the right side. Though constructed of the same material as the old mill, the schools shared none of its charm. They were simple, utilitarian one-story buildings. Claire turned again, intending to circle the block. "This is the high school," she said with a gesture toward the third nondescript brick building. "That's where I work."

"You're a teacher?"

Claire wondered why that seemed to surprise John. "You mean Glinda didn't tell you?" Her grandmother must be slipping. Normally she regaled visitors with exaggerated stories of Claire's accomplishments, including the fact that Claire was the head of Hidden Falls High's FCS department. Glinda frequently neglected to mention that Claire held that position because she was the one and only faculty member in FCS.

The reason for Glinda's uncharacteristic reticence was soon clear. "Actually, I wasn't at the house very long before you arrived," John explained. "Glinda didn't even have time to show me the room I'm renting."

Claire raised an eyebrow. "And you took it, sight unseen? You're a brave man."

"Not really. I knew it would be better than Motel Lumpy."

As he described his experiences at the no-star hotel, Claire continued around the block. Her tour was complete; all she needed to do now was take them home. Casually, she looked at the sports fields that filled half the block. Though none of the teams was practicing this late in the day, judging from the speed with which the ball flew across the net, two women were in the midst of a hotly contested tennis match. Claire smiled, thinking of the times she and Ruby had been just as competitive. Her smile faded when she saw the sole figure on the basketball court. His prowess was far less than the women's, for not a single ball landed inside the hoop. Few came close.

Claire slowed the car. "That's one of my students," she explained as she pulled to the curb and lowered the window on John's side. "Ryan!" The teenager approached the car, his expression wary. Like many of his classmates, he was uncomfortable with his recent growth spurt, not quite knowing what to do with the additional inches and the oversized hands and feet. Privately, Claire called it the Growing Puppy Syndrome.

"You left your jacket at school," she told the boy. "If you need it before Monday, I can get it for you."

"Thanks, Ms. Conners." Though his words were addressed to her, Ryan's eyes were focused on her passenger. "I'll be okay. I figured that's where it was."

Though there was no real need to introduce them, something in the boy's expression caused Claire to say, "John, this is Ryan Francis. Ryan, Mr. Moreland. He bought Fairlawn."

Ryan's lips twisted into a scowl. "Like I didn't know that. Everybody in town knows about Mr. Money Bags and his fancy car."

Claire blinked in surprise at the unexpected hostility. Other than normal teenage moodiness, Ryan had always been a model student. She couldn't imagine why he was reacting this way.

"Ryan!" Claire said nothing more, letting her voice convey her disapproval.

"Sorry, Ms. Conners." He took a deep breath before he said, "It's a pleasure to meet you, Mr. Moreland."

The words were polite; the tone was not.

What was it about this town? John settled back in the seat, trying not to let the teenager's blatantly bad manners annoy him. Why should he care? He didn't have to prove anything to anyone. He was, after all, John Moreland. And yet he couldn't dismiss the boy's sullen expression any more than he could ignore a mosquito buzzing around his head. A pest. That's all it was. It would be easy to ignore Ryan, if he were the only one. But, even though Claire had not remarked on it, John had noticed the number of people who had watched them drive around town. Their faces had betrayed curiosity and something more, something close to mistrust.

That made no sense. Why would the people in Hidden Falls be wary of him? Renovating Fairlawn could only be good for the town. John had worked on more job sites than he could count, and he'd never before encountered this reaction. Was it, he wondered, the difference between a city and a small town, or was it something specific to Hidden Falls? Perhaps it was what Angela would call "bad chemistry."

John turned slightly. It was far more pleasant to look at Claire than at the rundown neighborhoods. Even if the rest of the town wasn't convinced, Claire seemed to have overcome her initial disdain and accepted him. That was good, since they'd be seeing each other regularly while he was in Hidden Falls.

Fate had a strange sense of humor, arranging for him to board in the lovely Ms. Leaving's home. Though John would have preferred the relative anonymity and greater privacy of a hotel, that hadn't been a possibility. He'd make the best of the current situation. There were advantages, John had to admit. After all, most hotels didn't have owners like Claire. Enthusiastic, intelligent, attractive.

Attractive? Why should he care that long, dark hair framed an almost perfect face? Why should he care that those deep blue eyes could sparkle with amusement or flash with anger? John didn't care. He wasn't looking for a romantic relationship. This was business, pure and simple. Claire knew that. That was why she kept trying to promote the town. But surely she could see just how hopeless Hidden Falls was. Even if he renovated it, the town was too far from a major population center to sustain the new shops. That was probably the reason the big box stores decided not to build here. Turning Hidden Falls into a thriving metropolis would be like turning that kid who'd been trying to shoot baskets into an NBA star: an unlikely proposition.

Half an hour later, as he took his first taste of dinner, John smiled with pleasure. At least one thing about Hidden Falls wasn't depressing. The food was excellent, the surroundings equally pleasing. The Conners' dining room was elegant with nary a *Wizard of Oz* poster in sight.

"Glinda, this soup is delicious." It was thick and satisfying, the perfect meal for a cool day. "If you don't mind, when I hire a chef, I'll have him call you for the recipe."

"It was Claire . . ."

"A chef?" Claire began to speak at the same time as her grandmother. "You're the first person I've met who has a personal chef."

"Nonsense." Glinda laid down her spoon and smiled, first at Claire, then at John. "I have a personal chef. Her name is Claire."

So cooking was one of the skills Glinda had alluded to earlier. John gave Claire an appraising glance. "I stand corrected. The soup is delicious, Claire." He emphasized her name and smiled at her. "What's in it?"

"Various vegetables. Mostly carrots, but some onions and potatoes too." She passed him the basket of freshly baked bread as she asked, "Will you be advertising locally for your chef?"

"If I did, would you apply?"

She shook her head. "I already have a job. I was just curious."

John suspected that Claire had reverted to her role as town promoter. It wouldn't be fair to let her think he'd seriously consider hiring someone who lacked the needed expertise. "I doubt anyone in Hidden Falls has the background to run a hotel restaurant," he said.

"Hotel?" It was Glinda who posed the question. "I don't understand."

Claire gave her grandmother a quick smile. "It appears that the rumor mill was wrong for once. It sounds as if John is planning to turn Fairlawn into a hotel, not his personal residence."

"That was my plan." With "was" being the operative word. John wasn't certain that the plan still made sense. "I envisioned a small, very luxurious hotel where stressed-out executives and their spouses could come to relax."

"You picked the perfect place," Glinda said, her face brightening. "Hidden Falls is very restful."

That was one way to describe it. "Moribund" was another. John took a bite of bread to delay having to respond. He wasn't certain whether the town was worse than he'd remembered or whether it was simply the boy's rudeness and the suspicious looks he'd received this afternoon that had made him start to question his decision.

"Do you think the townspeople would welcome a hotel and its guests?"

Glinda nodded vigorously. "Of course. We're all friendly."

"That's true," Claire said. John's expression must have betrayed his skepticism, for she added, "If you're thinking about Ryan, he's only a boy, and he's not representative of the whole town."

"Ryan Francis?" Glinda leaned forward slightly. "He's had a rough time."

Before her grandmother could continue, Claire interrupted. "Let's not gossip. John's not interested in everyone's life story."

That was true. He wasn't the least bit interested in most of Hidden Falls' residents. He didn't care about Ryan Francis and the difficulties in his life. But Claire was different. Though he'd recognized the "caution" sign she had erected when she'd told him about her parents, John couldn't stop thinking about the fact that Claire's mother and father had put their careers before their child. His own family situation wasn't perfect. The fact that he saw his father no more than once a year was proof of that. But at least John had grown up with one parent.

For a few minutes as they finished dessert, a creamy pudding that Claire assured John was at least moderately healthy, the conversation turned to upcoming events in Hidden Falls. John listened and tried to respond appropriately, but all the while he could not shake the feeling that he'd made a mistake. It wasn't an irreparable one, he told himself. Even though he now owned Fairlawn, nothing was forcing him to renovate it. He could do as the previous owners did and leave it empty. That was it. He'd call Angela and tell her to start looking for a new project, something in an urban area. At least there he wouldn't be surrounded by suspicious residents and a woman whose story touched him far too deeply.

"I have a fair number of calls to make," John said when he'd eaten the last bite of pudding. "I don't want to be rude, but I'd appreciate it if you could show me my room." He'd brought his bags in from the car but, at Glinda's urging, had left them in the front hall until after dinner.

"I'll clear the dishes while you take John upstairs." Glinda winced slightly as she spoke to her granddaughter. "My knees are bothering me today."

John doubted that, and—if Claire's expression could be believed—so did she. This was like the tour of the town that Glinda had insisted they take. She obviously wanted John to spend as much time as possible with Claire. Wouldn't Glinda be horrified if she knew how her plan had backfired?

John followed Claire up the stairs to the third floor, noticing how the stairway narrowed for the final flight and how the oak risers changed to less expensive pine. When the house was built, the top story was probably used for nothing more than storage. Now the converted attic would be his, at least for tonight.

"Here it is." Claire opened the door and allowed John to enter the room first. Whatever he'd expected, it wasn't this. The sloping ceiling and deep dormer left no doubt that this had once been an attic, but any resemblance to a Spartan storage area was gone. Though the dark pine floor could have made the room seem somber, the pale yellow walls gave an illusion of sunlight. The contrast was continued in the dark furniture with lemon yellow upholstery and a matching yellow spread on the bed.

John looked around, nodding appreciatively when he saw the padded window seat and the well-appointed desk. The room was neither masculine nor feminine. It was . . . He searched for the word. Welcoming. The room welcomed him much as Fairlawn had, and that was a surprise.

"Be careful under the eaves," Claire cautioned. "They're not meant for someone your height."

John nodded, then turned to face her. "The room is beautiful. Your interior designer did an excellent job." Another surprise. He hadn't expected the combination of such elegance and comfort in Hidden Falls.

"I enjoyed living here," Claire said, "but I thought I should be closer to Glinda. I didn't hear her when she fell one night." Apparently uneasy with the subject, Claire led the way to the bathroom. "There are extra towels in the closet."

When Claire had descended the stairs, John reached for his cell phone. It was time to tell Angela that he'd decided to abandon this project. It had been foolish to venture so far from his area of expertise. He was an urban renovator, not a hotel magnate.

John was ready to push speed dial when he stopped. Leaning back in the chair, he let his gaze move slowly around the room. It was amazing, truly amazing. He rose and walked around the room, touching the furniture, enjoying the tactile sensation of running his fingertips over the upholstery. When he returned to the desk, John pulled out his laptop. This was twice now that Hidden Falls had thrown him curve balls, shattering his expectations. The first had been the feeling of homecoming that he'd experienced the first time he'd seen Fairlawn, the same feeling that enveloped him each time he was there. And now he had the sense that this room embodied everything he wanted to accomplish in his hotel. It was luxurious without being ostentatious, different enough from most people's homes that it felt exciting and new, but still comfortable.

The discouragement he'd felt earlier vanished, replaced by the urge to begin work. John booted the computer, realizing that he had no intention of calling Angela. While he wouldn't go so far as to claim this was his destiny, continuing the Fairlawn project once again felt right.

Creating a hotel would be a challenge, but it was something new for him to try. It would be one of those "stretch goals" the business journals touted, designed to make people continue to grow by taking risks. John liked that. Fairlawn would give him the opportunity to prove that he could succeed in a new area. That challenge was the reason he was staying here, not the all too attractive woman downstairs.

"Have you started your guest list yet?" Claire asked her grandmother when she entered the kitchen. Glinda had loaded the dishwasher and was filling the sink with water.

"Are you sure you want to do this? It'll be a lot of work."

Claire reached for a dishtowel. "After all the birthday parties you gave for me, I'd like to have one for you." She picked up the soup tureen and began to dry it. "Besides, seventy is a milestone."

"It means I'm way over the hill." Glinda punctuated her words with a wry smile.

"Seventy is a major accomplishment," Claire countered, "definitely worthy of a celebration." She had been thinking about hosting a birthday party for Glinda for close to a year, although she hadn't broached the subject with Glinda until a week ago. "Mom and Dad have already arranged their schedules so they can be here."

Glinda looked up from the pan she was scrubbing. "They have?" More than anyone, she knew how difficult it was for her son and daughter-in-law to coordinate their time off.

Claire nodded. "It's too bad that Fairlawn won't be ready. That would be the perfect spot for your party."

"So, postpone it."

"Nope. But we'll have your seventy-fifth there."

"And your wedding reception."

They were back on familiar territory. "Don't hold your breath for that. I told you there were no candidates for the position of husband."

Glinda let the pan slide back into the dishwater. "I may

not have to hold my breath," she said, her smile one Claire knew all too well. "Just open your eyes, honey. John Moreland is definitely husband material."

Claire busied herself drying the ladle. "What makes you think that, other than the fact that he's rich and handsome?"

"He's attracted to you, and you are to him." When Claire started to sputter a denial, Glinda held up a soapy hand. "I may wear glasses, but I'm not blind. I know what I saw."

"That's nonsense, Glinda, and you know it. I just met the man."

"There's such a thing as love at first sight."

"In fairytales, maybe, but not in Hidden Falls. Besides, John is all wrong for me. You heard him. He has no plans to stay here, and I have absolutely no intention of leaving Hidden Falls."

Glinda leaned back against the sink. "You may not have a choice, if the school closes."

Claire wasn't sure which was worse: discussing John Moreland's matrimonial inclinations or her own imminent unemployment. "Don't remind me of that. I'm working on my ostrich act." It wasn't easy, but Claire was trying not to worry. Her first priority was to get herself and her students through this school year. Surely summer was soon enough to face the unpleasant possibilities.

"I still think John came to Hidden Falls for a reason."

"He did: to renovate Fairlawn."

"Oh, Claire. You're putting your head in the sand over more than your job. John Moreland would be a good husband."

Claire tried not to sigh. Hadn't she told John that Glinda was persistent? The dishes would be finished in a couple minutes, and then she could escape. In the meantime, she might as well try to make her grandmother understand just how wrong John Moreland was for her.

"His job is terrible," she told Glinda.

As the water drained, Glinda glanced over her shoulder. "Why do you say that? He seems to enjoy it."

Claire's parents enjoyed their jobs, too. "It may be good for him, but it would be terrible for his family. You heard him say how little time he spends in his condo." Claire took a deep breath. "One thing I decided a long time ago is that if I marry and have children, they'll be raised by two parents."

An expression of pain flitted across Glinda's face. "I was wrong. I thought your father was the most stubborn person on earth, but you've outdone him. Why won't you listen to reason?"

As her grandmother launched into an argument they'd had more times than Claire wanted to count, she told herself that perhaps it was time to seriously consider moving in with Ruby. At least Ruby wouldn't harangue her about getting married, not even to someone as handsome, charming, and eligible as John Moreland.

Chapter Four

*S*he opened the door carefully, smiling when light from the hallway spilled into the room and revealed the rocking chair that had been hers as a child placed next to the hand-hooked rug from her grandmother. Pushing the door wider, she slipped inside. The mobile was still revolving, the octet of dolphins appearing to jump through the ocean spray. Soft music, reminiscent of waves, filled the room. She took a deep breath and tipped her head to the side, listening. Though the strains were beautiful, nothing could compare to the sweetest music of all, the sound of her baby's even breathing.

Tiptoeing, she approached the crib, then stood there, transfixed. Was there anything on earth as wonderful as a sleeping child? The infant stirred, tiny eyes opening, pudgy arms reaching toward her. A love deeper than anything she'd ever known rushed through her, and her heart overflowed with happiness as she gathered the child into her arms. "Mommy's here," she whispered, pressing a kiss onto the small head.

At the sound of heavier footsteps climbing the stairs, she turned. "It's all right, John. You don't have to tiptoe. The baby's awake."

Brrring. Brrring. Claire reached out to silence the alarm clock. She didn't want to wake up, not this morning when she'd been in the midst of a wonderful dream. Refusing to open her eyes, she tried to recapture the magic. She'd been upstairs in the nursery, and John . . .

John! Claire's eyes flew open and, with a muffled cry, she pushed herself to a sitting position. That wasn't a wonderful dream. It was a bizarre hallucination. How odd that she'd dreamed of holding a baby! Her baby. John's baby. It was even more bizarre that it had felt so right. Claire switched on the overhead light. Perhaps two hundred watts would bring her back to reality and dispel the strange sensations that even now made her face flush. It was only a dream. Nothing more. It would be foolish to assign any significance to it.

Freud was wrong. Dreams weren't always signals from the subconscious. Glinda used to say that a nightmare could be caused by eating too much pepperoni pizza. Of course, this hadn't been a nightmare, and Claire hadn't had any pepperoni pizza last night. Still, the fact was, it was a dream, just a dream. It wasn't as if she secretly wanted John's baby. She wasn't ready for motherhood, and she most certainly was not considering marrying John Moreland.

Claire flung open her closet door and stared at her clothes, trying to decide what to wear. She wouldn't think about the dream. She wouldn't remember how happy she had felt, holding the baby in her arms, or how the sound of John's footsteps had filled her with contentment.

Stop it! Claire grabbed her favorite navy skirt and a white blouse. She had many more important things to occupy her, things like the future of the school, Glinda's birthday party, the color nail polish she'd buy. They were all far more important than a silly dream. Of course they were.

An hour later, Claire was sitting in the faculty dining room, sipping a cup of coffee in the vain hope that it would settle her nerves, when Ruby arrived. Though Claire had gotten to school fifteen minutes later than usual, Ruby was even tardier.

"You look happy this morning," Claire told her friend as she glanced at her clothing. While Ruby frequently wore what she called her signature color, today she'd outdone herself. Both her sweater and skirt were red. "Last night's date must have been good."

"Oh, it was." Ruby reached for the coffee pot. "I don't know why I waited so long to go out with Steve."

Claire did, but chose not to remind her friend that she had sworn off men and dating ever since her less than amicable divorce a year earlier. Instead, she asked, "How was dinner?" Ruby had been thrilled by the fact that Steve had invited her to an exclusive restaurant perched on a hill.

"Aerie was incredible! I can see why they named it after an eagle's nest. The view was spectacular, and the food . . ." Ruby smacked her lips, provoking a burst of laughter from one of the other teachers. She lowered her voice conspiratorially. "I brought you a menu." With a flourish, she handed it to Claire.

"Thanks." Claire opened it and sighed. If the food was as good as the descriptions, it was no wonder Ruby had smacked her lips. "You just made my day." Claire had a small collection of menus that she used in her Creative Cooking class, helping students create fine dining experiences. The annual dinner that the teens prepared for their parents was the culmination of a year of planning.

Ruby stirred a second teaspoon of sugar into her coffee. "You may not be so happy when I tell you what Steve said."

"He didn't like the food?"

Ruby shook her head. "It has nothing to do with dinner." Though there were only a few teachers left in the room, she lowered her voice again. "Steve told me that John Moreland filed for a zoning variance for the hotel."

"So, what's the big deal?" While the Town Council, of which Steve was a member, was notoriously conservative, Claire couldn't imagine that they'd deny John's request. She wasn't even sure why Steve had felt the need to mention the variance request to Ruby.

"Did you know that John plans to put in a helicopter pad?"

As the warning bell sounded, Claire swallowed the last of her coffee. "Why would he need one? Choppers are noisy, and he said Fairlawn would be a restful place."

"Steve said he gave them some story about guests being in a hurry and needing easy access to the hotel. The rest of the council believed him, but Steve thinks John wants to keep his guests from ever seeing Hidden Falls."

"Why on earth . . . ?" Claire's voice trailed off as she remembered John's expression when they'd driven through town and his obvious discomfort when she'd asked about his plans for renovating the old downtown area. "If he does that," she said, "there won't be much benefit to the town."

Ruby nodded. "The council tried to pin him down. They asked whether he was going to hire local staff and buy food here. Steve said he was vague on the hiring part, but he claimed that the food had to be fresh, so it would come in by helicopter."

"That's awful!" Claire rinsed her mug and laid it on the drainer. "The local farms' produce is far fresher than anything he'll get in New York." As she followed Ruby into the hall, she muttered, "I thought John was going to help us."

Ruby shook her head slowly. "Nothing's going to save the school, but I did hope we'd get some tourists in town. The merchants could sure use the business."

They had reached Ruby's classroom. Before her friend could enter it, Claire said, "John is coming back today." He had been dividing his time between Hidden Falls and a second project in New Jersey. "You can bet that I'll have something more than the weather to discuss with him. I've got to get him to change his mind before the council votes."

Though Claire tried to control her anger, she was still seething when the school day ended. What a fool she'd been! The truth was, John hadn't misled her. She'd been the one who'd jumped to conclusions. He'd never said anything about expanding the project beyond Fairlawn. It had been Claire's wishful thinking that had imagined a renovated downtown. John had no more intention of doing that than he did of . . . Unbidden, the memory of her dream and the way he'd smiled when he'd looked at the baby flashed through Claire's brain. She wouldn't think about that. Instead, she picked up her cell phone and called Glinda.

"I have an errand to run," she told her grandmother, "so I'll be a little late." Claire did not like confrontations, but she saw no alternative. She had to do everything she could to help her town, and that meant persuading John Moreland to consider the future of Hidden Falls.

When she reached Fairlawn, Claire saw John measuring the *porte cochère*. Alerted by the sound of tires on the gravel, he straightened his back and approached her car. Claire tried not to wince. It wasn't fair that he was so handsome, and it most definitely wasn't fair that, instead of focusing on what he was planning to do, her treacherous mind replayed the dream. *Why, oh why, couldn't she forget that? It was only a dream.* Claire climbed out of the car and forced a smile onto her face.

"This is a pleasant surprise," John said. Though she doubted he'd say the same thing when he learned the reason for her visit, she kept smiling. "Have you come to see the progress we've made?"

"Among other things," she admitted.

"I'll be glad to give you the grand tour in a couple minutes." He turned toward the house and called, "Finished, Rick? It's time to go."

A few seconds later a dark-haired man emerged from Fairlawn. Though not as tall as John, he was almost as handsome, with roughly hewn features that Claire thought of as belonging to the quintessential cowboy. What was a cowboy doing in Hidden Falls, New York?

"Claire, I'd like you to meet Rick Swanson, the best architect in the country." John clapped the man on the shoulder. "Rick, this is Claire Conners."

Rick's grin was engaging. "I'm glad to meet you. I have to admit that John has made me salivate with stories of your cooking."

"I guess there are advantages to boarding with an FCS teacher. If you'd like to join us for dinner tonight, we'd be glad to have you."

Rick glanced at his watch and frowned. "I'd like to stay, but I've got a little boy waiting for me. Another time, maybe." He headed toward a black SUV.

"Tennis on Tuesday?" John asked before his friend could climb into the vehicle.

"You bet!"

As Rick drove away, John led the way toward Fairlawn's front entrance. "The little boy is Rick's son. His wife died last year, and he doesn't like to leave Josh with a babysitter any more often than he has to."

"I understand." And Claire did. Glinda had been careful either to schedule her community events and meetings at times when Claire was in school or to have them at their house so that Claire would not need a babysitter.

"You need to look beyond the grime." Though John was gesturing toward the interior of Fairlawn, Claire realized it was advice she could apply to her life. She'd ignore the less than perfect aspects and focus on the positive ones. Right now her focus was on something else that was far from perfect: John's plans. While she wanted to talk about them,

Claire's instincts told her it would be better to let him continue his tour. He might be more amenable to suggestions after that. Besides, she was curious about the interior of the house. Glinda had told her of its former beauty, but it had been closed for half a century. That had to have taken a toll.

"This is obviously the dining room," John said as he pushed open a set of double doors, revealing a spacious and, to Claire's surprise, completely furnished room.

She looked around. Years of neglect had left the furniture so covered with dirt that she could only speculate about the patterns carved on the chair and table legs. The crystal chandelier was similarly coated, and though Claire guessed that the drapes were once pale gold, they also could have been green or even cream colored. The carpet was best described as muddy.

"I'm trying to decide whether to keep the big table or have individual ones." John pointed toward an imposing piece of furniture. "This sideboard definitely stays, if only for atmosphere."

Claire agreed but returned to his earlier statement. "Don't guests expect to have their own tables?" That had certainly been her experience and was one of the challenges that restaurants faced when large parties made reservations. Tables for four had to be pushed together to accommodate groups, with results that were not always perfect. Claire recalled one time when an exuberant party had shifted the tables so much that a plate had literally fallen through the cracks. She and her fellow students had dubbed it "The Grand Canyon Event." If John was expecting large parties, keeping the formal dining table might be a wise choice.

"Individual settings are more common," he admitted, "but I stayed at a castle in Scotland a couple years ago where we all ate at the main table. It felt like we were part of the family rather than guests. That was only an illusion, of course, because we paid handsomely for the privilege of staying there."

"As will your guests." Although he hadn't discussed proposed room rates, John had made it clear that Fairlawn would be an exclusive property, well beyond the means of the average Hidden Falls resident.

John inclined his head in assent as he opened the doors into what had once been the main parlor. "This is too formal," he said, gesturing toward the long settees that flanked the fireplace. "I want to have small conversation areas here."

Picturing the room with half a dozen groupings of chairs and tables, Claire nodded. She continued nodding as John led her through the rest of the house, discussing his plans. There was no doubt that he'd spent a lot of time thinking about Fairlawn and that his ideas were sound ones. Most of them, that is.

"So, what do you think?" he asked when they had descended the back staircase and were once again outdoors.

"It will be beautiful," Claire said slowly, "and I'm sure your guests will enjoy it."

John's forehead furrowed. "I hear reservations in your voice. What are they?"

Taking a deep breath, Claire reminded herself to keep her anger under control. She was as much to blame as John. She was the one who'd conjured the pipe dream. "I heard a story that I hope isn't true." Claire took another breath and exhaled slowly, following the technique she had been taught for quelling stage fright. It wasn't stage fright she was feeling now, but that didn't mean she had no need to calm herself. "I heard Fairlawn was going to be self-contained and that your guests would have no contact with the town. According to the story, you even plan to bring them in by helicopter."

As John nodded, a lock of hair fell onto his forehead. Instinctively, Claire's fingers longed to brush it back the way she'd brushed the baby's hair in her dream. *Stop it! That was a dream, nothing more!*

Oblivious to her internal conflict, John said, "Most of that is true. I can't imagine guests having any need to go into town."

"Not to shop or simply look around?" Claire tried to keep her voice even. There was no reason to antagonize him. Perhaps he hadn't considered all aspects of his plans.

They had walked to the back of the building, the site of the formal gardens. Though they were in sore need of weeding and pruning, it was not difficult to imagine how beautiful they'd once been. John gestured toward a wrought-iron bench. With a courtesy that she had thought extinct, he waited until Claire was settled before he took a seat next to her.

"I don't want to be rude," John said, "but why would anyone want to visit Hidden Falls? It has nothing to offer my guests."

"It could." Surely he could see that. The man was a master at turning rundown neighborhoods into highly desirable ones and at finding such creative uses for old warehouses that sections of cities once destined for the wrecking ball became magnets for both commerce and tourists.

"If you're thinking about Westby Green," he said, referring to one of his recent projects, "the situation is vastly different here. Hidden Falls is not a candidate for renewal. To be blunt, there's nothing to draw people to it."

"It was a beautiful old town."

John shook his head. "That may have been true a hundred years ago, but it's not the case now." The look he gave Claire seemed faintly pitying. "I know this is your home, but you're seeing it from an emotional view. You need to be practical."

Claire wasn't certain which irritated her more, the pity or the fact that he was resorting to stereotypes, calling her an emotional woman. Men had emotions, too, much as they might want to deny them. And women, contrary to John's apparent misconception, were not ruled by their feelings.

"Not everything can be measured in dollars and cents," she told him, her voice steely.

"In my world, that's the only measure."

Claire stared at him for a moment. Though at some level, she had known that, hearing John admit it still came as a shock. "Then I'm glad I don't live in your world. It must be a pretty empty place if you calculate everything's—and everyone's—value that way."

A frown crossed John's face. "You're making me sound heartless."

"No, I'm not," she retorted. "You're the one doing that. You're the one with the really messed up set of values."

John rose to his feet and glared down at Claire. "I'm a businessman," he said. "A good one. I make decisions based on facts."

It was a fact that superior size frequently provided both physical and psychological advantages. That was undoubtedly the reason John had chosen to stand. He'd been taught to create every advantage he could. There was no doubt that, looming over her as he was, John Moreland was a formidable presence. Claire not impressed. She might not be a multi-millionaire, but she'd taken the same college course. Refusing to let him intimidate her, she leaned back on the bench, her posture deliberately casual. "How's this for a fact? Guests on vacation tend to spend money more freely than they do at home. They are also happier with their vacation destination if it provides them the opportunity to buy things they wouldn't find in their usual shops."

John raised one brow, his expression faintly supercilious. "Two facts for the price of one." He was baiting her, trying to embarrass or anger her into an emotional retort. Claire knew that and refused to answer. Instead, she raised her own brows and gave him what she hoped was a look of regal disdain.

"Fine," John said at last. "I'll have a small gift shop at Fairlawn."

If he thought that would placate her, he was wrong. The shop he envisioned would be stocked with merchandise carefully chosen and helicoptered in. Hidden Falls would play no role. "It's not the same thing," Claire said as calmly as she could. She couldn't let him see how deeply she felt about this. "Our ancestors were hunters, and we've inherited some of those instincts. Part of the fun of buying things on vacation is hunting for them." The day Claire's professor had presented that theory had been an "aha!" moment for her, as she recalled how satisfying it had been to buy items in Paris, London, and Singapore, even though similar items might have been available closer to Hidden Falls.

John was clearly not impressed with the hunter theory. "I know you love your home," he said, another frown marring his face. "It's an admirable trait, but the fact is, I'm the expert here. I know how to renovate buildings and how to please a wealthy clientele."

With a supreme effort, Claire kept her hands from fisting at John's patronizing attitude. "I won't dispute that, but the fact is," she said, echoing both his words and the tone with which he had delivered them, "you know nothing about small towns. As for hotels, I'd even venture that your only experience with them is staying in them."

The barb appeared to hit, for John's frown deepened. "I can learn," he said shortly.

Claire didn't doubt that. "But will you?" she asked. "When you look at Hidden Falls, do you see the people who live here or just dollar signs? Do you think about anything other than the bottom line?"

"Of course I do."

"I wish I could believe that."

John balled his fists as he watched her drive away. He had been called many things in his life, but this was the first time anyone had called him heartless. Grabbing his key ring, he locked the back door, then strode to the front, his steps failing to dissipate the anger.

Heartless! The word echoed in his mind. She didn't understand. Of course he worried about the bottom line. That's what prudent entrepreneurs did. They worried about dollars and cents. But it wasn't the only thing he thought about. John hit the "unlock" button on his remote with more force than necessary. He thought about people. Of course he did. He thought about his friends. Rick had been his buddy forever, and there was Angela. He and she were more than business associates. Business associates didn't go to dinner, plays, and art shows together, any more than business associates played tennis every week. John shook his head, acknowledging the truth. Plenty of business associates did exactly that. But this was different. Of course it was. It was true that Rick and Angela were both deeply involved in his work, but that was coincidence. Pure coincidence.

John slid behind the steering wheel and switched on the engine. A quick look at the clock told him he had an hour before dinner. Forget that. He had no desire to see Claire Conners or listen to that barbed tongue of hers any time soon. He wasn't heartless. He was prudent, pragmatic, and highly successful. Though there was still work to be done on Fairlawn, he could do it from home. That was both prudent and pragmatic.

Picking up his cell phone, John told Glinda he'd been called to New Jersey and wasn't sure when he'd be back. It was a lie, but at least he knew there would be no beautiful women in his condo accusing him of being heartless.

He wanted to leave Hidden Falls. That was definite, and yet something he couldn't explain kept John from heading toward the highway. The direct route was a left turn on Forest. Instead, he took a right onto Mill Street and drove slowly past the buildings that his many-times-great-grandfather had built. Although he wouldn't go so far as to say that Claire was right, John had to admit that the town must have been attractive at one time. The mill had graceful lines, and the similarly styled building that had once been the company store was pleasing to the eye, as were the boarding houses. A hundred years ago, this would have been a pleasant street to stroll. But now?

John frowned. It wouldn't work. He had never believed in the "if you build it, they will come" theory of urban renewal. Every project he'd undertaken had been in a metropolitan area with a built-in supply of potential customers, residents, and tenants. Hidden Falls was different. Though John could envision the mill as a small shopping center with a couple restaurants facing the river, that wouldn't be enough. Who would be foolish enough to drive to an out-of-the-way place with no other attractions just to shop or eat lunch, especially with the high cost of gas? No one, or at least not enough people to make the businesses profitable. Even if all of Fairlawn's guests patronized the shops and restaurants, they wouldn't be able to sustain the businesses. The storeowners would struggle just to remain open. As for the cost of the initial renovations, John saw no way to recoup them. Developing this part of Hidden Falls made absolutely no sense. It was a crazy idea, one based on emotions, not facts.

Making a quick U-turn, John headed toward the highway. He had never let his emotions rule him. He certainly would not do it this time. It didn't matter that his family had once lived here. It didn't matter that he'd felt an unexpected connection to the buildings his ancestors had created. It didn't even matter how persuasive Claire Conners could be. He wouldn't waste another minute looking at the old mill and dreaming. John was not a dreamer. He was a practical, action-oriented businessman.

Though he should have turned onto Forest, John continued north on Bridge, then cut over a block onto Chestnut. He wasn't going to Claire's house. He wouldn't do that. He was simply driving this way to remind himself of how hopeless the town was. Hidden Falls' lack of potential was a fact, and John liked facts. But as he passed the schoolyard, he saw a solitary figure shooting baskets. The rude kid. *Ryan. What was his last name? Something that could have been a first name. Francis, that's right.*

The kid had looked at him as if he, John Moreland, was pond scum. Though it shouldn't have mattered, John had to admit that that had bothered him, just the way Claire's obvious disdain had gotten under his skin. He couldn't change Claire's opinion, but Ryan Francis might be different. Impulsively, John parked the car and climbed out. "Can I join you?" he asked when he reached the basketball court.

The teenager eyed him suspiciously. "Why?"

Biting back a glib explanation, John decided on the truth or at least a portion of the truth. "I just had an argument with someone, and I want to work off some steam." As the boy continued to stare at him, John asked, "Didn't you ever feel that way?"

"Yeah." Ryan's conversational skills appeared to consist of monosyllabic replies.

"So, can I join you?"

"Yeah." With obvious reluctance, the boy passed the ball to John.

John dribbled a few times, then tossed the ball, missing the basket by more than a few inches. "I guess I'm out of practice." The fact was, he hadn't played since college. "I'm better at tennis."

"That's a rich man's sport."

Encouraged by the length of Ryan's reply, John ignored the barb. He dribbled again, then grinned as the ball touched the rim and slid smoothly into the basket. It was surprising how satisfying it was to watch that ball fall through the hoop. Maybe he wasn't as out of practice as he'd thought. Maybe the day would start to improve.

"How'd you do that?" For the first time, the kid's words were not snarled. Yep. John's day was improving.

"The coach claimed it was all in the wrist. Like this." He demonstrated.

Ryan watched carefully, then tried to imitate John's motion. Though he missed again, this time the ball was closer to the net. "So," Ryan asked as he dribbled, "is it true you're gonna turn Fairlawn into a fancy hotel and restaurant?"

"Yeah. Got a problem with that?"

"Nah, it's cool." Ryan tossed the ball back to John. "I figure my mom can have her birthday dinner there."

John kept his eyes focused on the ball. There was no point in telling Ryan that the restaurant would not be open to the public. "It'll be a while before it's ready," he said mildly. "Let's try this again."

Half an hour later, John climbed back into his car, convinced of two things. Number one: both Ryan Francis' basketball skills and Hidden Falls' downtown were in need of improvement. Number two: though he might wish otherwise, John was not the man to make those improvements.

"If I bring the DVD, will you make popcorn?" Claire asked without preamble when Ruby answered the phone.

"Sure. What's up?" Though Claire thought she had hidden her frustration, Ruby knew her so well that she had sensed it.

"I'll tell you when I get there. Now, what do you want: drama, mystery, or comedy?"

"Comedy, definitely."

"Good choice."

When she'd picked up the video, Claire turned north onto Maple, heading for Ruby's apartment. It was instinctive, looking at the school as she passed it. Ruby had admitted that she did the same thing every time she drove by. At this hour, the sports fields should be empty. Claire glanced at them, her foot easing off the accelerator when she saw that there were two figures on the basketball court. Ryan and . . . *Why was John Moreland there?* He'd told Glinda he had a project in New Jersey. Some project.

"I tell you, Ruby, I don't trust the man." Claire settled onto the charcoal gray couch that provided a pleasing contrast to the red walls of her friend's apartment.

"Aren't you overreacting?" Ruby pulled a bag of popcorn from the freezer and poured it into a measuring cup. "He's a respected businessman."

Claire shook her head, denying both of Ruby's statements. "He lied from the beginning." She held up her hand, turning down one finger as she said, "He claimed his name was John Baxter. He pretended he was buying Fairlawn as a residence. He didn't say he was trying to exclude the town from everything, and he told Glinda he had to go home, but he's still in Hidden Falls." By the time she finished, Claire had four fingers folded.

"I can't comment on the last one, but as far as the others are concerned, it seems to me that John told the truth—just part of it." Ruby poured corn into the hot air popper.

"That's still lying." Raising her voice to be heard over the blower, Claire continued. "The man obviously doesn't believe in 'the truth, the whole truth, and nothing but the truth'."

"This is business, not a court of law."

Claire didn't want to listen to Ruby's sensible statements. "Speaking of courts, I saw him shooting baskets with Ryan when he was supposed to be on his way to New Jersey."

"You lost me there." While she waited for the corn to pop, Ruby leaned against the counter. "Just how does that make John Moreland a villain?"

"I don't trust him. He uses people, and though for the life of me I can't figure out what use John Moreland would have for Ryan, I'm afraid he's going to hurt him. The kid doesn't need that."

"Relax." Ruby grabbed a supply of paper napkins. "You worry too much. If I had a man like John Moreland living in my house, I'd be figuring out a way to make the situation permanent." Before Claire could respond, Ruby said, "In fact, if you're not interested, I might see if I can generate any sparks."

"Ruby!" Claire felt the blood drain from her face. *Ruby and John?* Unbidden, the memory of her dream resurfaced. Claire took a quick breath, tamping down those traitorous images. "I thought you'd sworn off marriage."

"That was last week."

"Oh." Claire nodded slowly. She didn't care who John Moreland dated. Of course she didn't.

Chapter Five

John's mood had not improved by the time he arrived home. It was late; he hadn't eaten dinner; traffic had been backed up on the Garden State Parkway for no apparent reason. This definitely was not the kind of day to make a man smile with pleasure. He grabbed his bags from the trunk and punched the elevator button. Things would look better once he was inside the condo. The view of the Manhattan skyline never failed to soothe him.

It did tonight.

While he waited for the microwave to work its magic on freezer cuisine, John paced the floor. He didn't want to think about the delicious meal that Glinda and Claire had undoubtedly enjoyed, or the fact that he should not have left Hidden Falls so abruptly. With only two weeks until the Town Council made its decision on his zoning variance, he should have been there, shaking hands and doing whatever it took to persuade the council. Instead, he was watching a frozen dinner revolve in a microwave.

There was no freezer cuisine in the Conners' household. John knew that, just as he knew that he shouldn't have let

Claire's criticism sting. He was the expert. He knew what made sense—business sense, common sense, every kind of sense. She was an FCS teacher. What made her think that those credentials gave her the right to tell him he was wrong, that he ought to broaden the scope of his project to include that dismal downtown? Claire's expertise was in creating incredibly delicious meals, not in renovating old buildings.

Despite her allegation to the contrary, John could—and would—make Fairlawn a successful hotel. It wasn't as if he had to do all the work himself. So what if he wasn't an expert in the hospitality field? He'd hire a manager, someone with a proven track record running properties like Fairlawn.

John scribbled a note on one of the pads that he kept in every room, close at hand, should inspiration strike. This wasn't inspiration, just a reminder to begin the search for a manager as soon as the variance was approved. He'd show Claire a thing or two. By the time he was done, her disdain would change to admiration. She'd be a first-hand witness to John Moreland's expertise. She'd call him . . .

Heartless. John shuddered as the word seemed to reverberate throughout his body. He should have been able to dismiss Claire's angry comments. *Consider the source,* he'd always told himself when he'd received criticism. Unfortunately, when he did that this time, it only intensified the stings, and that increased his annoyance. It was ridiculous to care so deeply about Claire Conners' opinion, just as it was ridiculous that he'd spent the drive home thinking about the abandoned mill building, envisioning ways to turn it into a money-making enterprise. Ridiculous. Positively, absolutely ridiculous.

When the microwave binged, John pulled out his meal, resolving that he would concentrate on something—anything—other than Hidden Falls and its annoying inhabitants. Idly, he picked up the paper. There it was. That was the answer.

The next morning, he reached for his phone and pressed speed dial.

"'Morning, Angela," John said when the familiar voice answered. "Did you see the paper last night?" When she muttered something about being too busy to read it, he continued. "There's a review of what's supposed to be an excellent Italian restaurant in Morristown. Could I interest you in having dinner with me tonight?" Inspired by both his mediocre meal and the desire to think about things other than Hidden Falls, John had made reservations as soon as he'd read the review. By some stroke of fate, there had been one table open.

"They're reported to have the best cannoli in the state," he told Angela when she seemed to hesitate, perhaps because the weatherman was forecasting rain. Angela had never liked driving in the rain.

"Cannoli," she said with an exaggerated sigh of pleasure. "You always did know the way to my heart."

"I thought it was your stomach we were discussing."

This time the sigh held a hint of exasperation. "Where's your romantic side, John?"

"If I ever had one," which he doubted, "it's MIA. Now, do you want to have dinner with me tonight, or are you going to leave me with no choice but to eat all that fine Italian food alone?"

"I wouldn't do that to you, and you know it. Besides, you also know I never pass up a good cannoli."

John spent the day working on the final paperwork for the Greeley project. Though paperwork was far from his favorite part of his job, at least this was the last packet he'd have to prepare for Greeley. Hidden Falls would be easier, but . . . John frowned. He wasn't going to think about anything related to Hidden Falls today, or tomorrow, or the next day, either. Next week was soon enough to ensure that his variance was approved.

By the time he slid into the car that evening, John was smiling. The day had been better than he'd expected. Not only had he finished the paperwork, but his conversation with his mother had been remarkably pleasant. Either she hadn't seen the picture of his father with Janet, the third Mrs. Henry Moreland, or she wasn't admitting it. In either case, John was glad not to have been subjected to one of Mother's tirades. And now, with that obligation fulfilled, he was ready for an evening of mouth-watering food and stimulating conversation.

Two hours later, John stifled a yawn.

"Rough week?" Angela asked.

John nodded. It had been, although not in ways that should have made him yawn.

"Want to talk about it? You know I'm a good listener."

This time he shook his head, trying not to notice the hurt expression on Angela's face. It was true. She was a good listener, and in the past he'd bounced ideas off her. Though she wasn't an official part of his business, as his realtor, she knew more than most people about his projects. And as his friend, she'd listened and offered good advice over the years. That was why he invited Angela to so many social events. He enjoyed her company, her insight, and her conversation.

Tonight was different. Tonight, for the first time that he could recall, John found himself wishing the evening were over. Why had he chosen a restaurant whose service was described as leisurely? It was true that the food was as good as the review claimed. The soup was delicately flavored, the pasta cooked to perfection, the fish so tender that it almost melted on the fork. No one could have improved on it, not even Claire.

John tried not to frown. He didn't want to think about Claire. Hadn't he told himself that he wouldn't think about her? But it appeared that his brain hadn't been listening, for thoughts of Claire insinuated themselves into the fabric of

the evening's conversation, forming a pattern—an unwelcome pattern, he told himself—in the otherwise plain weave.

When Angela mentioned the flower arrangements, John
recalled the day he'd first spoken to Claire, when she'd been
pilfering daffodils from Fairlawn's garden. When Angela
complimented the chef on the soup, John remembered that
soup had been the first of Claire's creations that he'd tasted.
Worst of all, when Angela told John a story about one of her
clients, John found himself stifling another yawn and wishing it were Claire who sat opposite him. That was ridiculous.
Why would a man willingly seek a woman with a viper's
tongue for his dinner companion? *Because,* a voice deep inside him whispered, *she's not boring.* And, though he could
not explain the reason, tonight he found Angela boring.
Would the evening ever end?

The next morning John punched another speed dial button. "Hey, buddy," he said when Rick answered, "I got back
earlier than I'd expected, and I've got some ideas I'd like to
run by you."

"It's Saturday, John," Rick said. To his surprise, in the
background John heard the raucous laughter that accompanied children's cartoons. It *was* Saturday. "Unlike you,"
Rick continued, "I don't work 24/7. I have a life."

And, if Claire was correct, John did not. "Sorry to interrupt." Rick had switched their tennis matches to Tuesday so
that he could spend the entire weekend with his son.
"How's Josh?"

There was a moment of silence, as if Rick were trying to
compose his reply. "No change," he said at last. "The new
doctor said that's to be expected, but it sure wasn't what I
wanted to hear." John heard Rick's sigh and knew that he
was probably looking at the boy who'd been so traumatized
that he hadn't spoken a word since his mother's death. "Let's
change the subject." Rick's voice was husky.

John nodded, wishing there were something he could do to help his friend, but feeling helpless. If the experts couldn't break through the wall Josh had erected, what hope did a layman like John have? He nodded again before he realized that Rick couldn't see his gesture. A different subject. That's what Rick had requested. Not work, not Josh. Surely that wasn't too much to ask. John frowned when his mind remained blank, and he clenched his fist as memories of Claire's words haunted him. He wouldn't admit that she was right. It wasn't true that his life consisted of work and nothing else. But if it wasn't true, why was he having so much difficulty carrying on a simple conversation with his best friend?

"I had dinner with Angela last night," he told Rick. "That new Italian restaurant in Morristown."

"How was it?" It was surely John's imagination that Rick sounded as if he were grinning. There was nothing amusing about dinner with Angela.

"The saltimbocca was good."

This time it wasn't John's imagination. Rick laughed. "I'm glad I met Claire."

"Claire Conners?" *Why on earth was Rick talking about Claire?*

Another peal of laughter. "Do you know more than one Claire?"

"Of course not." One was enough. More than enough. "What made you think of her? We were talking about dinner with Angela."

"I hadn't thought it possible," Rick said, his voice once again sober, "but it seems that miracles do happen."

First Claire. Now miracles. Rick wasn't making any sense. "What is wrong with you?" John demanded. "You sound like your brain is addled."

"Be with you in a second, Josh." Rick's words reminded

John that this conversation was impinging on Rick's time with his son.

"Sorry, Rick." John started to apologize.

"Don't be. You've made my day. I never thought I'd see it—John Moreland in love."

The man was definitely addled. "In love? I'm not in love with Angela."

"No one said you were." The smug satisfaction in Rick's voice made John want to punch him.

"You just did."

"Wrong. I said you were in love. The lady in question is not Angela. It's Claire."

If he hadn't been wearing a headset, John might have dropped the phone. *In love with Claire? Impossible!*

"It's good of you to make time for me, Mr. Ferguson." Though she would have called him Clyde under other circumstances, Claire knew that the president of the Town Council liked formality when he was acting in an official capacity. Since she wanted his help, she'd play by his rules.

"It's my pleasure, Claire. What can I do for you?" He gestured toward an empty chair in the room that normally functioned as the office of the Ferguson Pharmacy. Since membership on the Town Council required only a few hours a week, not enough to justify an office or full-time employees, Claire had long suspected that it was prestige rather than the small stipend that motivated citizens to run for the council.

The look she gave the president was serious. "I have some concerns about John Moreland's proposed zoning variance."

"Why?" Clyde Ferguson peered over the top of his half glasses. "It'll increase the tax base. We need more commercial property." That was the response Claire had expected.

"I agree, and I'm not against granting the variance. It's

just that I'm worried that having Fairlawn as a hotel won't help us as much as it could. Mr. Ferguson, I think there should be some conditions attached to the approval."

He leaned forward, as if he were interested. That was a good sign. "What kind of strings do you want?"

"You know they're going to be hiring staff. I think a certain number of the new hires ought to be from Hidden Falls and that some percentage of the goods they buy ought to be from local merchants."

Clyde Ferguson leaned back in his chair, his expression telling Claire he was considering what she'd said. "Your argument is compelling," he said at last.

"I'm glad to meet you, Mr. Ferguson." Though the words were commonplace, John meant them. If the rumors were accurate, this man's opinion could sway the Town Council.

"Call me Clyde," the council president said, pointing at an empty chair.

"All right, Clyde." John settled into the chair, then leaned forward slightly, as if he were going to confide a secret. It was a tactic he'd learned, not in school, but by watching his father. "I won't take much of your time. I just want to be certain you have all the information you need for my variance."

"Your paperwork is complete."

There was something in the man's voice that made John ask, "Do you anticipate problems?" A week ago, John would have said that he couldn't imagine any, but that had been before he'd learned how strongly Claire felt that the project should encompass more than Fairlawn. If she had approached the council, John was afraid they'd listen. After all, Claire Conners was a resident and—from what he'd observed—a respected one. That was the reason he was here today, spending time he couldn't afford with a small town bureaucrat.

Clyde shrugged. "I have to admit that this is the first variance request we've received. That means there are no precedents."

John fixed his most earnest expression on his face. "Having Fairlawn as commercial property will be an asset to the town." *The best thing to happen to Hidden Falls in half a century.* Though he was tempted to tell the president of the Town Council exactly that, John said only, "I've checked the tax records, and it appears that Fairlawn's assessment will equal that of the mall. That increased tax base is good for everyone in town."

The man was silent for a moment, obviously considering John's statement. At last, he peered over his glasses. "Your argument is compelling," he said.

"I've got to hand it to you, Claire," Ruby said as she opened her container of yogurt. "You're providing Hidden Falls with more entertainment than we've seen in years."

The two women were in the faculty dining room. Because it was unusually crowded today, they'd accepted the fact that they'd eat their food standing up. Claire pulled her meal out of the microwave. "Entertainment? What's that supposed to mean?"

"Steve told me that you talked to him and everyone on the council."

"And exactly what is entertaining about that?" Claire stirred the broccoli-cheese chowder, hoping it would cool enough to eat before her lunch hour ended. "I just want to make sure they consider all aspects of the proposed zoning variance."

Ruby didn't mean to be annoying. Claire knew that, but her friend's Cheshire Cat grin was irritating. "What's got everyone buzzing is that John has been to see the same people, usually just a couple hours after you. Folks are calling it the Tag Team."

Wonderful! It was bad enough that she had John Moreland living in her house four or five days a week and had to listen to Glinda singing his praises the days he wasn't there. Now it appeared that the town was getting involved. Claire did not want her name linked with John's in any way. "We are not a team."

"I know that. That's what makes it so funny."

"You must have a very strange sense of humor, Ruby Baker. I don't find it the least bit amusing." Though Claire had talked to John more times than she wanted to remember, trying to convince him that he needed to help the local economy in ways beyond simply paying real estate taxes, he'd remained as obstinate as the first time she'd broached the subject. The project was going to be Fairlawn, nothing more.

Ruby took another spoonful of peach yogurt before she replied. "It is funny, Claire. There you two are, an attractive man and woman, sharing the same house, but on opposite sides of a political battle. This could be a TV sitcom."

Claire fixed her steeliest glare on Ruby. "You may be my best friend," she said, "but there are times when I want to strangle you. It's probably just as well that we aren't rooming together."

"It's too late for that."

Claire blinked in surprise. Had Ruby found another roommate? "Too late? Why?"

"It wouldn't make sense for you to move for such a short time."

"What's in that yogurt?" Claire asked. "Whatever it is, it seems to be having a deleterious effect on your gray matter. You're not making sense today."

Ruby gave Claire another of those smug grins that irritated her. "If I were a betting woman, which I'm not, I'd bet that you'd be married by the end of the year."

"Married?" Claire sniffed the empty yogurt container, convinced that the contents must have spoiled.

"Yes, married, as in 'I do' and 'happily ever after'." Ruby's smile widened as she lowered her voice to a conspiratorial whisper. "Married to John Moreland."

Impossible!

Claire spooned the Chicken Marengo into a serving bowl, then carried it and the rice into the dining room. On days when John wasn't with them, she and Glinda ate in the kitchen, but Claire had insisted on more formality when they had guests. She had also insisted that there was no need for Glinda to help her prepare the meal. Glinda's responsibility, Claire had announced, was to entertain John. Admittedly, that was a bit dangerous, because you could never predict what Glinda would consider entertaining, but it was still better than having to make casual conversation with her obstinate guest.

Ever since that day at Fairlawn when John had made it clear that he had no interest in the town of Hidden Falls and that he would do his best to ensure that Fairlawn's guests had no reason to leave the hotel grounds, things had been strained between them. Oh, there had been no more hostilities, but the politeness was forced. Claire couldn't speak for John, but for her, the last two weeks had seemed endless. Between trying to convince John and, when that was unsuccessful, lobbying the Town Council members, Claire had the impression that each day had lasted at least thirty-six hours. Tonight the waiting would be over, for tonight the Town Council would announce its decision.

"Are you worried, John?" Though Glinda smiled, Claire saw faint lines of strain between her eyes. Why was Glinda worried? As she'd told Claire countless times, her life and Claire's would not change significantly, regardless of the decision. It was John who had the most to lose.

Claire tried not to frown at the possibility that her grandmother was a turncoat and supported the enemy. John was not the enemy, she reminded herself. They shared at least one common goal, because they both wanted Fairlawn to prosper. The problem was that John wanted nothing more, while Claire did.

"Worried about what?" His voice was even; it was only the mischievous sparkle in his eyes that told Claire he was teasing Glinda. Another thought assailed her, one as unappealing as the idea that Glinda was on John's side. Was it possible that he knew how entertaining the townspeople found his and Claire's lobbying efforts? Was this all a game to him? No, it couldn't be. The man was far too serious to be playing.

"I thought you might be concerned, because tonight's the big night," Glinda said as she passed the bread.

"I've no reason to worry." It was surely only Claire's imagination that he sounded smug. "My project will benefit Hidden Falls."

Not as much as it could. Not as much as it should. Claire took a bite of bread, chewing slowly as if she were evaluating the blend of herbs that she'd used in place of the more traditional garlic. Perhaps if she kept chewing, the angry words that even now threatened to burst forth would remain unspoken.

"An excellent dinner, Claire. As always." John's words seemed sincere. He was, she had to admit, unfailingly polite when he was with Glinda, a fact that her grandmother mentioned at least twice a day, normally in the context of what a fine husband John would be. Ryan's mother was equally complimentary. She had stopped Claire in the supermarket one afternoon, telling her how thrilled she was that John played basketball with her son whenever he was in town. Claire, who hadn't known the extracurricular activity had been more than a one-time occurrence, had been surprised, even more so when Mrs. Francis had gushed about how wonderful it was that Ryan had a positive role model. Role model wasn't a term Claire would have used to describe John Moreland. Stubborn, opinionated . . . There was no point in thinking about that today.

"Thank you," Claire said, acknowledging John's compliment. He smiled. It was ridiculous, really, the way a simple smile could change a man's face. Harsh planes softened and what had been handsome became . . . breathtaking. As hackneyed as the word was, it was the only way she could describe the effect that John Moreland's smile had on her. For an instant, their differences were forgotten. Instead of thinking about tonight's vote and the impact it would have on Hidden Falls, Claire wondered what it would be like, sharing a table with John every day, seeing that smile every morning, hearing that voice every evening. Unbidden came the memory of the dream that, despite her best efforts, she could not forget. Though it had not recurred, Claire could still recall the joy of holding her baby and seeing John in the doorway. That was bad enough, but then there was Ruby's preposterous allegation that Claire was destined to marry him. *What an absurd idea!*

"Claire, dear, are you driving or is John?" Her grandmother's question brought Claire back to the present. When John raised an eyebrow, Glinda said, "We're all going to the council meeting. You didn't think I'd miss that, did you?"

For the first time since Claire had met him, John appeared surprised.

"Er . . ." He reached for his glass and took a sip of water. "I didn't realize there'd be others."

Glinda chuckled. "This is the most excitement Hidden Falls has had in years. Why, the only thing that will be more fun will be planning Claire's wedding."

Weddings! Claire cringed.

* * *

The number of cars in the parking lot should have been his clue, but even that hadn't fully prepared him. When they entered the school auditorium that was serving as the site of tonight's council meeting, John was shocked by the number of people already seated. Hidden Falls, it seemed, was not like New Jersey where driving was normally a solitary pursuit, and those SUVs in the parking lot had carried more than one person. This wasn't what he'd planned. He hadn't expected an audience, and, even after Glinda's warning, not one of this magnitude.

Keeping his most businesslike smile fixed on his face, John looked around the room. It appeared that Claire's grandmother hadn't been exaggerating when she'd said that the town was fascinated by his plans for Fairlawn. There were well over a hundred people in attendance, not the five person Town Council he'd expected.

It wasn't a problem, John told himself. Not really. He had argued his case in front of hostile boards and won. This group wouldn't be hostile, and if there was an audience, well . . . it wouldn't affect the outcome. There was no reason to feel uncomfortable, just because this was unexpected. It was simply another reminder of how different Hidden Falls was from the cities where he usually worked.

It wasn't just Hidden Falls. There were so many "firsts" on this project. It was the first time he'd planned to create a hotel, the first time his on-site accommodations had been a private house rather than a hotel, the first time he'd been accused of being in love. John's smile slipped. *In love!* He wouldn't think about that absurd allegation. Rick was out of his mind; that was the only explanation for his claim. Still. . . .

As he greeted the council members, John made an effort to recall the townspeople's names. That was preferable to thinking about Claire and how awkward the past couple weeks had been. The argument they'd had had been bad enough. He could have dismissed that, but ever since Rick had pronounced those ridiculous words, John had been almost tongue-tied around Claire. *How absurd!* He wasn't a teenager with a crush on the prettiest girl in school. He was a grown man who could have his choice of women. There was no reason, absolutely no reason, to feel this way.

He wasn't in love with Claire. Of course he wasn't. It was true that he thought about her more than he should. It was also true that he found himself noticing little things about her. Tonight, for example, he'd seen that she was wearing pale pink nail polish. John could not recall ever noticing a woman's nails, polished or not, and he knew for a fact that he'd never once wondered whether a woman's toe nails were painted. Until tonight, that was.

As he responded to another resident's question, John glanced around the room. There she was! Claire stood in one aisle, surrounded by a group of people he suspected were her teaching colleagues. His pulse began to race, and as it did, John clenched his teeth. This had to stop. These foolish feelings were the result of proximity, nothing more. Fortunately, there was a simple cure for proximity. He would move into Fairlawn tomorrow. Even in its current state of filth, even though it didn't have a functioning microwave, it would be preferable to living in the same house as Claire Conners. John was a businessman. He needed to focus on his project, not on a woman whose beauty kept him from sleeping and whose quick repartee was somehow more interesting than his career.

As he made his way to the front of the auditorium, John was pleased to note that the greetings were friendly. It seemed that the townspeople's initial distrust had faded. Surely that was a good sign. John wouldn't read anything ominous into the fact that he sat alone in the first row. That was probably protocol. After all, the others were observers, while John was a participant in tonight's meeting.

Clyde Ferguson rapped on the table, calling the meeting to order. "The first item on the agenda," he announced, "is John Moreland's application for a zoning variance." Apparently it didn't matter that the variance had been filed by JBM Enterprises. No one cared about the company; it was John who was newsworthy here.

The council president read the official petition, then cleared his throat. He was obviously enjoying his fifteen minutes of fame. "The council has reviewed the request," he said with an expansive gesture at the file folder he'd placed on top of the table. "We have also received comments from several taxpayers. Are there any additional comments before the council makes its decision?"

John looked at Claire. Although she had not said so, he suspected she had been one of the taxpayers who'd opposed his variance. Tonight, seated next to Glinda on the opposite side of the auditorium, Claire's eyes appeared to be fixed on Clyde Ferguson. She said nothing, nor did anyone else in the audience. Other than normal fidgeting and rustling, there was silence. *That was*, John told himself, *another positive sign.*

Clyde picked up the folder and withdrew a single sheet of paper. "The council has received a number of suggestions related to this particular zoning variance. Some," he said, looking directly at Claire, "were more viable than others."

Claire inclined her head slightly, a motion that John suspected was being observed by everyone in the room. *What was it*, he wondered, *that she had proposed?* Surely she hadn't suggested that the variance for Fairlawn be tied to renovations of the downtown area. For Pete's sake, he didn't even own those properties.

"All recommendations have been taken under due consideration." Clyde's satisfied tone confirmed that he was enjoying being the center of attention. "The council is now ready to announce its decision. Before we do that, we have a question for Mr. Moreland."

Though the use of his formal name raised John's hackles, he kept a polite expression on his face. He wouldn't do anything to alienate the council, or the town, for that matter.

"What is the question, Mr. Ferguson?" If Clyde could be formal, so could John.

"We wish to be certain that you recognize that Fairlawn is part of Hidden Falls."

"I do." John winced as the words conjured the image of a church, two gold rings, and a woman who looked disturbingly like Claire Conners wearing a long white gown.

"In that case," Clyde continued, "we will approve the zoning variance with one stipulation."

John nodded slowly, encouraging the council president to describe the strings they planned to attach to Fairlawn. Though he had hoped for approval with no modifications, dynamics were different here. Perhaps the Town Council felt the need to demonstrate its power. John hoped that, whatever the stipulation might be, it wasn't too onerous.

"Fairlawn is part of Hidden Falls," Clyde said. He looked around the auditorium, making eye contact with a number of people, heightening the suspense. "We want to ensure that the town is also part of Fairlawn."

John nodded again, not sure where this was headed. The platitudes were starting to sound pompous.

"We don't believe you'll find our contingency burdensome." This time Clyde turned toward the other council members, waiting for each to nod his agreement.

Though there had been the normal shuffling of feet and whispers while Clyde had spoken and the council had conferred, the room was now totally silent, the anticipation almost tangible. John took a deep breath, exhaling slowly. He could always abandon the project, he reminded himself. He did not have to agree to a ridiculous stipulation.

"We understand that you do not plan to make Fairlawn your permanent residence." Clyde continued to speak.

"That is true."

"We assume that means you will hire a manager to oversee the day-to-day operations."

"This is also true."

Clyde turned to the other council members. Once again, they all nodded. "Very well, Mr. Moreland. Your variance will be approved if you hire someone from Hidden Falls to be that manager."

John blinked. Surely the man was joking. Surely they didn't think he would agree to hire someone from this hick town in the middle of nowhere to run his multi-million dollar hotel. Surely they knew this wasn't legal. They couldn't force him to do something so outrageous. Why, Fairlawn would be doomed from the beginning.

"I don't . . ."

Before John could complete his sentence, Clyde Ferguson raised a hand, silencing him. "Allow me to finish. The council expects you to hire someone from the town as your manager. That someone is Claire Conners."

Chapter Six

W hat on earth was going on? John felt the blood drain from his face. It wasn't often that he found himself blind-sided, but this qualified as one Class A shock. He could understand the council asking him to hire some wait staff from the town, but this? Their suggestion—correction, their requirement—was ludicrous. There was no way he could agree to it.

John gripped the seat arm as shock turned to anger. Why had they done this? It made no sense. If he hadn't known how badly Hidden Falls needed the revenues Fairlawn would generate, John would have considered the possibility that the council was trying to sabotage the project. Either that, or they wanted to watch Claire fail. She was a great cook and a well-respected teacher. That made her the perfect person to advise the Gourmet Wannabes. It did not qualify her to run a luxury hotel. Perhaps the council didn't realize that. If this had been Claire's suggestion, they may not have considered it too closely.

John turned to look at her. Judging from her glassy-eyed expression, Claire was as shocked as he. The anger that had caused his hands to clench and his blood pressure to rise fifty points began to subside. Whatever else she might have done, Claire wasn't behind this ridiculous stipulation. Thank goodness! Beside the fact that an unqualified manager would doom Fairlawn, John couldn't imagine the two of them working together every day. Or could he?

Gritting his teeth, John rose to protest the decision, but before he could speak Clyde Ferguson opened his mouth. The council president peered over his half-glasses, his smile verging on a smirk. For some perverse reason, he was enjoying John's reaction. "Mr. Moreland, I suggest you and Ms. Conners discuss this. We will reconvene one week from today to hear your decision." Rapping the table with his gavel, he smiled again. "Meeting adjourned."

It seemed as if everyone spoke at once. "Great idea," John heard a man say. "Best thing the council ever came up with," a woman declared. "Wish I'd thought of it," a third added. Everyone considered it a brilliant solution. Everyone, that is, except John, and—if he was reading her expression correctly—Claire.

"What are you going to do, John?" A dozen people clustered around him, their curiosity overflowing. "Are you going to hire Claire?"

He inclined his head slightly in the gesture a public relations consultant had told him helped inspire confidence in an audience. Though John wasn't trying to convince anyone tonight, perhaps the gesture would transmit some of that confidence back to him. He certainly needed it, because at this point he didn't see any easy way out of the predicament. "The council will have my decision in a week," he said. "But first Ms. Conners and I need to talk."

Claire was on the opposite side of the room, surrounded by another group, all of whom seemed to be speaking at once. Though she kept a smile on her face, John recognized the signs of strain. He suspected some of those same signs were etched on his face. They needed to get out of here. But where was Glinda? John couldn't simply abandon her.

As if he'd summoned her, Glinda appeared at his side and laid a hand on John's arm. "It seems you and my granddaughter have things to discuss. Ruby will give me a ride home."

As politely as he could, John disengaged himself from the well-wishers and curiosity hounds and made his way across the room to Claire. "If you'll excuse us," he said as he picked up Claire's coat and helped her into it. Though he'd phrased it as a request, the townspeople must have heard the determination in his voice, for they cleared a path for him and Claire.

The night air was cool, almost cold. John took a deep breath, not sure which he appreciated more, the fresh air or the silence. Even Claire, who was normally not tongue-tied, said nothing, a change he attributed to the shock they'd both received. Once they were in the car, the words tumbled out. "I don't know what to say. I never dreamed they'd do anything like that. I did *not* suggest it."

The strength of her denials touched a spot in John's heart that he hadn't known existed. Somehow, for some reason, this woman thought it was important that he believe her. And he did. "I know you didn't do that. One look at your face told me you were as surprised as I was."

"Shocked is more like it."

"I know the feeling."

"I'm not sure you do," she countered. "The Town Council didn't tell you to quit your job."

John nodded silently. He'd been thinking only of what the decree meant to him. It hadn't fully registered how greatly Claire's life would change if they agreed to the ridiculous stipulation. Not that they would.

Though he couldn't have said why, John had headed west when he'd left the school parking lot. As they reached the outskirts of town, he pulled the car onto the shoulder. There were no houses here; no one would disturb them. It was time to talk.

"What happened tonight?" Perhaps she had more of an idea than he did.

"I'm not sure." John heard the bewilderment in her voice. "It's true that I thought you should hire local staff," Claire admitted, "and I told the council that. The difference is, I was thinking of wait staff and housekeeping, not your general manager."

John nodded. It appeared he and Claire hadn't been as far apart as he'd once thought. "I had planned to hire locals," he told her. "That is, if anyone's interested. Those aren't the best paying jobs in the world."

Claire shifted in the seat. Perhaps it was only John's imagination that she seemed more relaxed. He knew his tension was subsiding, now that they were talking. "Maybe not, but, as you've undoubtedly noticed, Hidden Falls isn't the most affluent area in the country. I venture to say you'll have more applicants than positions."

She was silent for a moment, and in the faint moonlight, John saw an emotion he could not identify cross her face. If he'd had to guess, he would have called it regret. Surely that was wrong. Claire had no reason to regret anything about Fairlawn.

"I never even considered the possibility that the council would think I should be the manager," she said at last.

Thank goodness. This was one more point where they were in agreement. "The position requires a specific background and training," he said mildly.

"I know."

"And," he added, "unless I'm greatly mistaken, courses in hotel management aren't required for a degree in education, even for an FCS teacher."

"That's true. They aren't."

It must have been John's imagination that Claire's voice held a hint of amusement. There wasn't anything even remotely humorous about this discussion.

"Given all that, I don't understand why the council thinks you know anything about running a hotel."

She turned and faced him, and this time there was no doubt. She was smiling.

"Because I do."

It had been too much to hope that Glinda would have gone to bed before Claire returned home. Instead, she found her grandmother and Ruby sitting in the kitchen, cups of steaming cocoa in front of them. The inquisition was about to begin.

"Where's John?" Ruby raised an eyebrow when she saw that Claire was alone.

"He said he wanted some time to think." Claire didn't blame him for that. The truth was, she wanted some time for reflection too. The evening had taken its toll. Now that the adrenaline rush had subsided, she felt limper than an overcooked piece of broccoli. "I suspect he's at Fairlawn, trying to decide whether the project is worth being saddled with me. Either that or calling his lawyer to figure out whether this is legal. My guess is John's going to cancel the whole project rather than deal with a Town Council that's overstretched its authority."

Glinda rose and poured cocoa into a third mug. "Now, my dear," she said as she placed the cup on the table and gestured toward an empty chair, "I'm sure John doesn't feel that way."

"Are you? Didn't you see his face when Clyde told him what the stipulation was?" If Claire had had to paint a picture of a man in shock, John Moreland would have been the perfect model.

"It's a brilliant solution." Glinda's eyes sparkled, and her smile was one of eager anticipation. Claire hadn't seen her grandmother this excited since the day she'd met Chuck Warren, the last man before John that she'd considered suitable husband material for her granddaughter.

"Brilliant in whose eyes?" Claire demanded. "Not mine and not John's, that's for sure." She took a sip of the cocoa, noting that Glinda had added a bit of cinnamon. Though she preferred cardamom, the cinnamon flavor was pleasing. "Whose idea was it, anyway?" A muffled sound made Claire look at the woman on her right. "Ruby, don't tell me you were behind this."

Ruby shrugged, as if her complicity were admirable. "You're perfect for the job, Claire. You've got the right background."

"I have a degree in hotel administration," she corrected, "but no practical experience. Fairlawn needs both if it's going to be successful."

"You could do the job," Ruby insisted.

"With no experience, it would be a stretch." Claire gave her grandmother an appraising look. "By the way, John seemed surprised when I told him about my major. You're slipping, Glinda. I assumed you'd given him my full pedigree." When she was in matchmaking mode, her grandmother wasn't shy about telling a prospective grandson-in-law every aspect of Claire's life.

"It didn't seem important."

"You're right; it's not important. I'm a teacher now."

Ruby laid her mug on the table and faced Claire. "I know you don't want to hear this, but that may not be true in a year. That's one of the reasons why working at Fairlawn is so perfect for you."

Claire closed her eyes as images of herself at Fairlawn began to dance through her brain. The large closet on the first floor would make an ideal office, allowing her to keep her finger on the pulse of the whole building. She could picture herself there, listening to the sounds of laundry carts being wheeled through the halls, dishes being stacked, phones ringing. Scents of flowers would mingle with the more pungent odors of starch and bleach. There was nothing as exhilarating as a smoothly functioning hotel.

Claire sighed as she forced her eyes open and herself back to reality. It was true that running a hotel had once been her dream. Both Glinda and Ruby knew that. But that had been a decade ago, when she'd still been at college. That had been before Glinda's mini stroke and Claire's decision to remain in Hidden Falls. That had been before she'd discovered just how much she enjoyed teaching.

Glinda pushed her glasses back onto her nose. "I won't tell you what to do."

Before her grandmother could complete her sentence, Claire said dryly, "I appreciate that."

"But," Glinda said, ignoring Claire's interjection, "I think you should consider it."

Ruby nodded. "It's the perfect solution."

They were wrong. "I doubt John would agree with that."

"Hey, Rick, did you get Josh to bed?" John settled himself on one of the sheet-covered chairs in Fairlawn's parlor and prepared for a long conversation. One good thing he could say about Hidden Falls was, no matter how far from civilization it sometimes appeared, the cell phone coverage was excellent.

"No problems tonight." How John wished he could say the same thing. After the slightest of pauses, Rick asked, "What's up?"

"There's a wrinkle in the Fairlawn project." A wrinkle the size of Mount Everest. Though it wouldn't affect Rick's work, John wanted to hear his friend's reaction. Unlike the residents of Hidden Falls, Rick would be on his side.

"Don't tell me the council didn't approve the variance, because I won't believe it. I've seen Hidden Falls. I know how much they need Fairlawn."

"You should have been here tonight. They didn't act as if they saw the same things you and I did." John explained what had happened.

"You're right. I wish I'd been there." John heard the muted laughter in his friend's voice. "It sounds like one of those priceless moments."

John leaped to his feet and began to pace, trying to tamp down his irritation. Rick was supposed to sympathize with him. Didn't he realize that? "I'm glad you find the situation amusing. I don't."

This time there was no doubt about it. Rick was laughing. "Oh, I do find it amusing to think of you and the lovely Claire being forced to work together. That will be better than anything on TV."

The conversation was not going the way John had hoped. "My job is not to provide entertainment for you and the citizens of Hidden Falls. My job is to turn Fairlawn into a resort and make money doing that. Lots of money," he added, in what he hoped was a subtle reminder that Rick owned shares of JBM Enterprises.

"You can always sue the council," Rick offered when he stopped laughing.

"Trust me, buddy. I already considered that. The problem is, even if I won, the Town Council could make my life miserable. There are lots of little things that need approval and some not so little ones, like building inspections. If I don't agree to hire Claire, my guess is that everything will happen so slowly it'll make glaciers look like speed demons."

"You could be right."

"I am."

John looked around the parlor, trying to envision it when the renovations were complete. He could picture guests mingling. He could almost hear their conversations and smell the mélange of perfume and colognes. He could imagine the new carpet and drapes, the pieces of period furniture. But, try though he might, he could not conjure the image of Claire working here.

It was strange. The first time John had seen her, he'd pictured her at Fairlawn. That had been part of what had convinced him to buy the property and turn it into a hotel. But the image of Claire that he'd had that first day had been different. She'd been a guest, not an employee. Claire, the general manager. As John's classmates used to say, That did not compute.

"Let me see if I've got this right." The humor in Rick's voice had vanished. "You're afraid you'll fail if the lovely Claire is your manager."

"Wouldn't you worry? You and I've worked hard to establish a reputation for excellence. I don't want to jeopardize that."

"Do you really think having the lovely Claire working there will lower Fairlawn's chances of success?"

"Precisely. And stop calling her 'the lovely Claire'."

"Yes, sir!" John heard the sound of heels clicking and knew that Rick was giving him a mocking salute. For years that had been their signal that John needed to back off. But how could he, when so much was at stake?

Rick's voice resonated with concern as he said, "Sounds like you're a little touchy tonight."

"Wouldn't you be?" John demanded. "The Town Council is trying to tell me how to run my business. I'm the expert, not them. I know how to pick a General Manager. They don't."

"But you said that TLC has the right background."

"TLC?" If Rick's goal was to annoy John, he was doing a first rate job.

"You're slipping, my friend." There was no ignoring the amusement in Rick's voice. "That's the acronym for the name you've forbidden me to use."

TLC. The lovely Claire. Of course.

"I thought you were my friend."

"I am."

"Then why are you trying to irritate me? Hidden Falls' Town Council has already done a stellar job of that."

It appeared that Rick had no intention of answering John's question, for he countered with one of his own. "Is it true that she has the background you need?"

"Yeah." And that had surprised John. "A degree from the Cornell School of Hotel Administration is impressive. It's one of the best places in the country to learn the hospitality business. But that doesn't change the fact that she has no experience."

"So, there's a risk. Let's face it, John. There's a risk in everything." The sudden sadness in Rick's voice told John he was thinking of his wife. For Heidi, living had been a risk.

Rick cleared his throat, then said, "It seems to me that you need to decide how important Fairlawn is to you. You can always walk away from it."

"I can." But as he hung up the phone, John realized that he didn't want to.

A business meeting. That's all it was. Claire repeated the words to herself as she stared at the contents of her closet. This wasn't a date, which meant there was no reason to be agonizing over which dress to wear.

She hadn't heard John come into the house last night and wasn't certain he'd even returned from Fairlawn until he descended the stairs for breakfast. Though the circles under his eyes attested to a sleepless night, his voice was as calm as if they were discussing nothing more than the weather when he suggested that they resolve "the issue," as he called it, on neutral territory. That neutral territory had turned out to be the most exclusive restaurant in this part of the state. Claire had no idea how John had been able to get reservations on such short notice, and she wouldn't ask. Today of all days she didn't want to be reminded of how much power the Moreland name wielded.

Somehow she'd gotten through the school day, and now she stood in front of her closet, unable to make the simplest of decisions. Which dress? The apricot silk whose mid-calf skirt swirled when she walked, the royal blue sheath that Glinda insisted made her eyes look like sapphires, or the black dress that Ruby had somehow convinced her to buy despite the astronomical price tag? They were all suitable for dinner at Roxanne's. The question was, was any of them appropriate for a business meeting?

When Claire's cell phone buzzed, she flipped it open and recognized Ruby's number.

"Wear the apricot," her friend said without preamble.

"How did you know I was . . . ?" Before Claire could finish her sentence, her door opened and Glinda slipped inside. "The royal blue," Glinda announced. And so, because she was in a mood to be contrary, Claire wore the black dress.

An hour later, she descended the stairs.

"Would a wolf whistle be allowed?" John asked when she reached the bottom.

The approving look in his eyes made Claire's pulse race. *This isn't a date,* she reminded herself. Still, she couldn't deny the fact that she was glad she'd chosen this dress. With its modestly scooped neckline and long sleeves, it could be described as demure. If, that is, you ignored the slit in the

skirt. Though not evident when she stood motionless, the slit
revealed flashes of leg whenever Claire walked. *There was
nothing wrong with that,* she told herself. After all, she had
well toned legs from all her jogging. The fact that John appeared to have noticed them made her pulse accelerate again.

"A whistle?" she asked sweetly. "In a business meeting?
Absolutely not."

"I was afraid of that." A mischievous grin crossed John's
face as he let his eyes move leisurely from the top of her
head to her black patent pumps. "Nice dress," he said at last,
silently telling her that she hadn't forbidden him to look.

Claire returned the favor, noting that tonight his frequently wind-tousled hair had not a strand out of place. The
fit of his charcoal suit was so perfect that it had to have been
tailor made, and she guessed that the deceptively simple
white cotton shirt had cost more than most of the suits in
Hidden Falls. From the carefully styled hair to the hand-
crafted Italian shoes, John Moreland's appearance spoke of
money. Lots of money. And yet what Claire saw was not the
expensive clothing, but the man who wore it. A man so
handsome that he made her heart beat faster, a man who
starred in her dreams more often than she wanted to admit, a
man she might be working with for the foreseeable future.

"Nice suit," she said simply.

John grinned in response, then held Claire's coat for her.
"Don't wait up for us, Glinda," he said. The way he was acting, Claire could almost believe this was a date. It wasn't, she
reminded herself. It was a business meeting. Nothing more.

"Did you get any work done today?" John asked when
they were settled in the car for the hour's drive to Roxanne's.

"Some," Claire said, "although I had a lot of distractions.
The kids all wanted to know if I was going to quit. As for my
colleagues, everyone seemed to have advice for me."

John chuckled. "That sounds like my day. I had a constant

stream of interruptions. I think everyone in Hidden Falls came up the hill today to offer their advice."

Claire suspected the townspeople's advice to John had been as unwelcome as she had found her colleagues'. "I'm sorry you were subjected to that, but people care about the town."

He shook his head slowly. "It's you they care about. Everyone sang your praises."

It was good that the car was dark and John couldn't see how a flush colored her face. "I'm really sorry about that." She could only imagine the stories he'd heard. "I've lived here almost my whole life, and everyone knows I won't leave, so they're a little too protective of me."

"Why won't you leave? With your credentials, it seems to me you could get a job anywhere."

It wasn't that simple. "Hidden Falls is where I belong," Claire said. No matter what Ruby or John or even Glinda said, she believed that. "My parents are both Sagittarians and love to travel. I'm more rooted." And where she was rooted was Hidden Falls. "Besides," she added, "Glinda needs me."

"She strikes me as pretty independent." There was no censure in John's voice, simply a statement of fact.

"She's almost seventy."

"Two generations ago that was old. It's not anymore."

Claire smiled. "You sound like Glinda. Speaking of whom, I thought I'd warn you that she put you on the guest list for her birthday party. You might want to invent an iron-clad excuse for refusing."

John flicked on the turn signal and exited the highway. "Why would I want to refuse?"

"I can't imagine you'd enjoy it."

Slowing the car, John looked at Claire. "There's a lot you don't know about me, including what I enjoy doing with my free time."

"I didn't know you had any of that."

"Believe it or not, Claire, I'm trying my best not to be a total workaholic."

Perhaps that was the reason John refused to discuss "the issue" while they dined. When Claire mentioned it, he simply said "later" and began to recommend items from the menu. "If you like escargots," he said, "Roxanne's are excellent."

They were, as were the roast lamb, the sautéed green beans, and the duchess potatoes. If Claire had tried, she could not have surpassed the meal, and she doubted even her most critical professor would have found any faults with the restaurant. The tables were set a discreet distance apart, allowing for private conversations. The linens were perfectly starched and ironed, the china the finest Limoges could offer, the crystal so thin that Claire shuddered to think what a single goblet had cost. Candles and fresh flowers on each table added to the ambience, an ambience of elegance and romance. Roxanne's was the perfect place for a first date.

This was not a date, first, last, or anything in between. Claire tried to remind herself of that with each course, but as the hours passed, it became more and more difficult, for John's behavior was not what she'd expected from a business meeting. He kept their conversation light, centering on the things they enjoyed. Claire learned that John was an avid tennis player, considered golf a necessary evil, and thought the perfect day included dinner in a fine restaurant. She told him about her popcorn and DVD evenings with Ruby and the pleasure she found in her after-school gourmet cooking club. Not once did they discuss anything related to Fairlawn or the Town Council's decree.

This was dating behavior, but they weren't dating. Of course they weren't. The only reason they were having this seemingly irrelevant conversation was that John was trying to assess how well they'd work together. If congenial conversation counted, they'd succeed. The problem was, working together involved a lot more than enjoying each other's company. There had to be mutual respect, and Claire wasn't sure John would ever accord her that. He was used to a traditional boss-employee corporate structure, while she thrived as a member of a team.

When they had finished their dessert and cheese courses and the waiter had refilled their coffee cups, John leaned forward, his blue eyes once more serious. "Do you have any suggestions about how we can solve our dilemma?"

Although she suspected it was a negotiating ploy, Claire liked his use of the plural pronouns, as if this would be a joint decision. It wasn't, of course. She knew that, and that was part of the problem. Claire took another sip of coffee before she said, "It seems to me that it all depends on you."

Throughout the day, though she'd tried to concentrate on her classes, Claire had considered the possibility of managing Fairlawn. If the circumstances had been different, it would have been a dream come true. But the circumstances weren't different. John was being forced into a situation that he obviously didn't like. He was a man accustomed to making his own decisions. Having a major one foisted on him had to rankle. It would be difficult enough working together, but knowing that she was there because of a fiat, rather than John's choice, would increase the friction between them. It would turn what could have been a dream into a nightmare. That was why Claire had made her decision. She would decline the position. She'd continue teaching, and John could hire the general manager he wanted.

John's eyes clouded as he shook his head. "I'm afraid you're wrong, Claire. It depends on both of us. Clyde Ferguson was one of the parade of people who came to Fairlawn today. He made it clear that if you refuse, the deal's off."

"Oh!" Claire felt as if she were in an elevator that had suddenly dropped three floors. The food she had savored just minutes before formed a lump in her stomach.

"Was that what you had planned to do?"

Claire nodded, still speechless as she tried to assimilate the fact that the Town Council's strings had become iron bands, linking her to Fairlawn and John. How could they? Why did they? Reasons were academic; what mattered was finding a way out of the dilemma.

John shook his head slightly, as if he'd read her mind. "Refusing won't work. Neither will lawsuits. So now, what do you think?"

It was odd. In all of her dealings with John, she had seen him as a decisive man, and yet tonight he was deferring to her. Why? Claire took another sip of coffee, trying to marshal her thoughts. "You're right. That does change things. So now my question becomes, how badly do you want to turn Fairlawn into a hotel?" Badly enough to work with a manager he hadn't chosen?

John was silent for a moment, and Claire sensed that he was weighing his words. "A month ago, I might have given you a different answer, but although I can't explain it, I find that I want it more each day."

As the waiter refilled their cups, Claire's thoughts whirled. Last night she'd convinced herself that the whole idea was preposterous. But today the reasons she ought to refuse kept being drowned out by images of herself at Fairlawn, handling the crises, the challenges, and the celebrations that were part of running a hotel.

"Do you want it enough to work with me, knowing that I have no experience?" she asked when the waiter was gone.

"Yes." The answer came without hesitation.

"You haven't heard my terms." That was something else she'd thought about all day. If she were to take the position—which she had been certain she would not—what conditions would she place on her employment?

"I want full authority to hire and fire, full purchasing power, and approval of the décor and menu."

John raised one brow as he gave her an appraising look. "Is that all?"

She shook her head. "I also want a five-year contract with my salary guaranteed for the whole period, regardless of what happens."

This time a wry smile accompanied John's words. "Are you afraid I'll fire you as soon as the variance is approved?"

Though Claire had considered that possibility, she had been more concerned about the high failure rate of small hotels and restaurants. "I'd be giving up a job I like," she told him, "and need some security in return." It wasn't a total bluff. If Claire's job at Hidden Falls High was eliminated, she could apply for one in another town. She didn't have to stop teaching.

John nodded. "I understand your terms and have a few of my own. But first I need to ask you a question. You can call it the million dollar question." He paused for effect. "Are you willing to give up your teaching position to run Fairlawn? As you said, teaching is something you enjoy."

That was another question Claire had pondered throughout the day. "I believe it's the right decision for Hidden Falls."

John didn't bother to hide his annoyance. "Forget the town," he said brusquely. "What about you? Is this the right decision for Claire Conners?"

"It could be," she admitted, "but I haven't heard your terms." Would he try to curtail her authority so much that she'd be little more than an assistant with a fancy title? She knew that happened more often than people wanted to admit, when companies gave women titles without responsibility or authority, simply to improve their EEO reports. Besides being an untenable position for Claire, that wouldn't be good for Fairlawn. If the hotel was going to succeed, the decision maker needed to be there every day. That was why John needed a general manager, a real general manager.

He shook his head as the waiter appeared to refill their cups. "I have no major problems with your demands, other than that I want to be part of the personnel and purchasing decisions. You'll have veto power, but I need you to listen to my opinions."

That was a reasonable request. Claire nodded. "What about décor and menus?"

"Same thing there. The actual renovation and all the exterior work—that includes landscaping—will be my decisions and mine alone."

Claire nodded again. "That seems fair enough."

Half an hour later, they'd ironed out a schedule that allowed Claire to teach for another year and had agreed on her salary as well as a plan for how they would work together.

"Do we have an agreement?" John asked when the conversation lagged.

"It sounds like it to me." As she pronounced the words, Claire was startled by the elation that flowed through her. The tension and indecision that had plagued her ever since she'd heard the Town Council's decree were gone, replaced by excitement and anticipation. It wouldn't be easy. She knew that. And yet she couldn't deny how right it felt. For the first time, she'd be able to use her education to its fullest as she helped make Fairlawn a successful hotel.

"Great." John signaled the waiter, scribbled his name on the check, and rose. "Let's go." Claire smiled. This was the John Moreland she knew. With the business meeting over, he saw no need to linger.

A minute later, they were outside, approaching his car.

The night was warmer than Claire had expected, the stars now hidden by a blanket of clouds. Still, it was not an evening for strolling, and she was surprised when John's steps slowed.

"Something's missing," he said. There was a note to his voice that she'd never heard before. If she had to guess, Claire would have said that he was uncertain, but that was unlikely. "Uncertain" was one adjective she would never apply to John Moreland.

"What's missing?" she asked. Surely they'd covered everything important. The details could be worked out later. Besides, they had an hour's drive back to Hidden Falls. If John thought of something they'd missed, they could discuss it in the car.

He took a step closer to her. Though they'd been walking side by side, now he faced her. "When I reach an agreement with colleagues," he said, "we always shake hands."

Claire pulled off her glove and extended her hand. Though she expected John to clasp it, he did not. Instead he looked at her hand for a second, his indecision palpable. Something was wrong. As Claire started to retract her hand, John moved quickly, closing the space between them. For a moment, he stood there, so close that she could hear his breathing and see the intensity in his eyes. Then, without warning, he pulled her into his arms and lowered his lips to hers.

Claire had been held in a man's arms before. She had been kissed before. But never before had it felt like this. John's arms were firm, his embrace making her feel both safe and cherished. His lips were soft, teasing hers with their gentle caress. As one of his hands stroked her hair, Claire moved closer, reveling in the way her curves seemed to fit into the angles of his body and the way empty spaces deep inside her that she hadn't known existed were filled by his nearness. She closed her eyes. For a moment nothing mattered but being in John's arms, feeling his lips on hers.

The night may have been cloudy, but Claire was certain this man had just given her the sun, the moon, and all the stars. It was magic. No other words could describe the wonder of John's embrace. Pure magic.

Chapter Seven

Claire tried not to frown as she looked at her watch. Would the impromptu staff meeting end before she had to leave for the cooking club? She had only twenty minutes, and staff meetings were rarely that short. When Gerry had called it, the teachers had assumed he wanted to tell them what had occurred at the School Board's meeting the previous night. But as he ambled into the room, Gerry's first words were, "Nothing new on the consolidation. The paperwork's still with the State."

He gestured toward the sheaf of papers that he was carrying. "This is a revised schedule for the rest of the year. Grades need to be in a day earlier than usual." A grin crossed his face as he added, "I think you all know why." The reason was one of the happier topics the staff had to contemplate: their administrative assistant's silver anniversary trip to Hawaii.

"I sure wish I was going," Ruby muttered to Claire. "It sounds so romantic."

"Hawaii with Frank?" Claire had never understood what Leah saw in her husband, but whatever it was, it had been enough for the marriage to last a quarter century. "Given that choice, I'd rather stay in Hidden Falls."

When Gerry dismissed the meeting a couple minutes later, making Claire wonder why he hadn't simply sent the schedule via e-mail, Ruby continued their discussion. "It's easy for you to be happy here. You're spending all your free time with John Moreland."

"That's business." As she pronounced the words, Claire felt the color rise to her cheeks. It hadn't always been business. What had happened in Roxanne's parking lot had not been business. It had been . . . The word "wonderful" was only one of many that came to mind. Claire fumbled in her purse, pretending to look for her card key. Why on earth couldn't she forget that kiss? It was clear that John had. Not only had he made absolutely no mention of it, but everything he'd done or said since that moment had been purely professional. Either he'd dismissed the kiss from his memory or he regretted it. It was only Claire—silly, silly Claire—who couldn't forget how wonderful it had felt to be held in John's arms, who even now could recall how sweet his lips had felt pressed to hers.

"Business?" Ruby didn't bother to hide her skepticism as she and Claire joined the queue of teachers filing out of the room. "Looks like *personal* business to me."

This was one topic Claire did not want to pursue. "What about Steve?" she asked, hoping that Ruby would forget she'd even mentioned John Moreland. "I thought you and he were serious."

Ruby shook her head. "Not any more. He told me we have different world views, whatever that means."

It was, Claire reflected, a good way to describe the differences between herself and John. Maybe it was because he thrived in urban settings, while she was content in a small town. Maybe it was because of the differences in their backgrounds. John was the son of a beauty queen and a mover-and-shaker, while she'd been raised by a woman whose measure of success was the number of her friends, not a rhinestone tiara or an impressive stock portfolio. The result was, Claire and John didn't see the world the same way. John viewed everything as a matter of dollars and cents; his goal was to make the most money possible from every project. But Claire, having been raised by Glinda, believed in the importance of helping others. Profit was secondary.

A sound suspiciously like a sniffle drew Claire's attention, and she realized that what mattered right now wasn't anyone's world view; it was the pain Ruby was feeling. No matter how lightly she appeared to dismiss it, Ruby was obviously upset that she and Steve had broken up. She wouldn't appreciate a hug here where the students could see her, but tonight was different.

"It sounds like time for another popcorn and DVD marathon," Claire announced. "We can have it at my house."

Ruby, who'd been accompanying Claire on her way to the Gourmet Wannabes, wrinkled her nose. "With John there? No thanks." Her wistful expression told Claire she would have welcomed the invitation otherwise.

"John's not living with us any more." As Ruby raised an eyebrow, Claire continued. "Being at Fairlawn is more convenient." At least that was what he had said. The fact that he'd moved out the day after The Kiss told a different story. John wanted their relationship to be business, nothing more.

"I see." Ruby sounded thoughtful. *What was it*, Claire wondered, *that she saw?*

It was a juggling act. That was the only way Claire could describe her schedule. Teaching and supervising the Gourmet Wannabes had kept her busy before John Moreland entered her life. Now working with him on Fairlawn filled every remaining moment, leaving her with little time to worry about what would happen to the school. And that, Claire reflected, was a mixed blessing. Even though both Ruby and Glinda insisted it was not her responsibility to save the school, Claire couldn't help feeling that she had to try.

Gerry had told them that politics was playing a greater role than he'd expected. Though Rockledge was centrally located and had initially appeared to be the logical site for the new school, the mayor of Bartonsville was lobbying to have it in his town. Hidden Falls, as the smallest of the three districts, wasn't under serious consideration. Claire wanted to find a way to change that. That was, she realized, part of her world view. But for this afternoon, she wouldn't think about the school. This afternoon was to be devoted to Fairlawn.

Though it was still early in the project, Claire had asked to be involved at every stage, even though that wasn't part of the typical general manager job description. John was already making structural decisions, and some of those would affect Claire. She had seen him and Rick walking through the interior, measuring each room and making copious notes, and she'd known that they were planning the renovations to what would be the guest rooms. While it might be a stretch to say that the shape and size of a room fell into the category of décor, Claire wanted to ensure that her ideas meshed with theirs.

The biggest challenge, John had told her, was fitting baths into the existing space. Wasn't it always? That had been the most difficult part of her attic conversion.

"Are you sure you want a tub here?" Claire stood next to John in one of the rooms that overlooked River Road. "I agree that a claw foot has style, but who'll use it?"

"It'll give the room a period look." John took a step closer to Claire and gestured toward the tall window with its ornate molding. They'd agreed to use glue chip glass so the bath would have light without sacrificing privacy. "It's all part of the same package."

Claire took a deep breath, regretting it an instant later, as the spicy scent of John's aftershave teased her senses. This was a business meeting, she reminded herself. There was no reason, no reason at all, why she should be standing this close to John or why she should care that his aftershave reminded her of how wonderful it had felt to be in his arms.

"A tub like that's impractical," she said, pleased that her voice betrayed none of the confusion she was feeling. "The bathrooms need to be modern with lots of light. I want to put a makeup mirror in each one, maybe even a shaving mirror in the shower."

John laughed, and somehow, though it was just a chuckle, it sounded low and intimate, like the kind of laugh a happily married couple would share. *Stop it, Claire! You're not married to John. He's all wrong for you.*

"I thought you were the purist," he said with another chuckle. "You're the one who told me all the room furnishings should be antiques or reproductions from the period when the house was first built."

"That's true," Claire admitted. "I think that's the right look for the bedrooms and the common areas. The bathrooms are different. They need to be practical." Claire gestured toward the space where John had said he wanted the free-standing tub. "People would rather have a whirlpool tub than a footed one, and women don't care about ambience when they're putting on eyeliner. A hundred-watt light bulb beats a pretty forty-watt fixture every time."

John held up both hands. "I surrender. We can put in spotlights if that will make the women happy. But what about the décor? I envisioned a seamless transition from the main rooms to the baths—sort of like the suite in your house. That decorator did a great job."

"Thanks." Claire almost laughed at the expression on John's face when he realized that she had been the decorator he had just complimented. Glinda was definitely slipping if she hadn't told him that Claire had renovated the attic as part of one of her school projects.

"I should have recognized that as your work," John said, his voice warm with approval. "No wonder I liked the room. Its style is different from what I think Fairlawn needs, but the ambience is perfect." He smiled as he looked at her. "I hope you don't get a swelled head, but that room helped convince me I should turn Fairlawn into a hotel. When I saw it, I knew that was the feeling I wanted here—a room that was welcoming."

Claire couldn't help smiling. She had tried so hard to make the suite both elegant and comfortable. Bubbles of happiness rose inside her at the realization that she'd succeeded. It wasn't simply that she had loved living there and that her professor had given her a good grade for the project. What delighted her was that John liked the room she'd created. Although he'd lived there for several weeks, he'd never said anything other than that the mattress was comfortable and there was plenty of hot water. That shouldn't matter. Claire hadn't renovated the room for him. She hadn't sought his approval. And yet, her heart beat faster at the thought that he'd liked it. That increased the odds that he'd like her plans for Fairlawn.

"Even though the lighting will be modern, I thought we'd use paint and wallpaper to give the baths an old-fashioned look. Sort of like this." Claire reached into her bag and pulled out a paper sample, propping it upright on the windowsill. "If we stick to the more traditional styles of plumbing fixtures and buy them in ivory rather than white, they'll blend with the bedrooms." Another foray into her bag produced an ivory ceramic chip. "See how they go together." Claire laid the chip next to the wallpaper, then started to step back so that John could view the effect.

It would have been a good idea, if she hadn't moved backward at the same time that he moved forward. As it was, Claire collided with a large, warm object. That large, warm object wrapped his arms around her to keep her from falling, and for the briefest of instants, she was back in Roxanne's parking lot. Claire felt the blood rush to her face as she remembered the touch of John's lips on hers and how sweet the kiss had felt. *Get a grip on reality,* she urged herself. At least John couldn't see her flaming face. As she shifted her weight, he dropped his arms.

"Perfect together."

Claire blinked. He was right. When she was in John's arms, nothing else mattered—not their differing world views, not their uncertain future. Nothing mattered but the sheer perfection of the moment. Though she hadn't admitted it, even to herself, Claire knew it was true. And, despite the way he seemed to distance himself emotionally, so did John.

"The combination is perfect," he said, pointing toward the wallpaper and ceramic samples she'd laid on the windowsill.

Of course! Claire cringed. *What an idiot she'd been! It was her decorating that John found perfect, nothing else.* When he'd put his arms around her, it had been a simple act of chivalry. He'd have done the same thing if an antique étagère had been about to fall. It was only Claire, foolish Claire, who had been affected by his nearness.

This had to stop. John had once accused her of seeing everything through the filter of her emotions. It appeared she was doing it again, and that had to stop. Immediately.

"Where's John?" Glinda asked an hour later as Claire set the table for two. Although he no longer occupied the attic suite, John occasionally ate dinner with them. Tonight would not be one of those nights.

"He had to go back to New Jersey." A fact for which Claire would be eternally grateful. By Monday when he returned, she'd have her emotions under control. She'd become Mr. Spock from *Star Trek* or, better yet, the Scarecrow from Glinda's beloved *Wizard of Oz*, a character without a heart. Either would be easier than continuing to remember things that should have been relegated to the darkest recesses of her memory.

"Aren't you glad you listened to me?" Glinda was wearing one of those smiles that made Claire afraid she really could read minds. How awful that would be!

"About what?" Surely her grandmother wasn't talking about John.

"About taking the job at Fairlawn. You're obviously enjoying it."

Fairlawn was a safe subject. "I am," Claire admitted. "It takes more time than I imagined, but you know it's what I've always wanted to do." If everything went according to schedule, Claire would do most of her preliminary work during the summer recess. Somehow she'd manage to fit the Fairlawn decorating and planning in during the school year. And then when school ended next June, she'd become Fairlawn's full-time general manager.

As she focused on thoughts of the juggling act that the next school year would bring, Claire barely noticed her grandmother's grin. Glinda reached across the table and laid a hand on Claire's arm. "You and John work together so well," she said, her smile broadening. "You're perfect together."

Claire shook her head. She knew what was perfect together. John had left no doubt about that.

John looked at the doorbell and hesitated. Today was one of those days when he wished he were a medieval knight, wearing a coat of armor. Odds were, he'd need it before the morning was over.

"Okay, Mother. What's up?" he asked when she'd opened

the door. With Leanne, there was no need for pleasantries. Besides, she was the one who'd wakened him, demanding that he come over immediately.

"It's your father." No surprise there. Though the divorce had been final for more than fifteen years and his father had remarried twice in the interim, his mother had not ceased her litany of complaints over Henry Moreland's treatment of her.

"What did he do now?" John tried to keep the weariness from his voice.

"He threatened to stop the alimony."

John shook his head slowly. "You know he can't do that, unless . . ." He gave his mother an appraising look. "You weren't stalking Janet, were you?" That situation had escalated to the point where John's father had gotten a judge to issue a restraining order.

"Of course not!" Leanne Moreland appeared indignant. "I can't help it if she and I just happen to shop in the same stores."

"Mother, you know you shouldn't do that." John took a long swallow of coffee. Thank goodness Leanne had given him her largest mug. He'd need it. "You ought to start dating again." It wasn't the first time he'd advised that, and he suspected that the response would be the one she'd given each time he made the suggestion that she needed to fill her life with something besides endless shopping. It was true she didn't need a salary, but volunteer work or an active social life might ease her bitterness.

"Why should I date? There's no one like your father."

Thank goodness. John took another sip of coffee, composing his words carefully. "You're a beautiful woman, Mother. I'm sure many men find you attractive." It was not a lie. Leanne Moreland had lost little of the beauty that had made her a finalist in the Miss America contest and had attracted Henry Moreland. She had been blessed with a bone structure that aged as well as the finest of wines.

Right now, that perfect face was scowling. "Your father put you up to this." She rose and pointed an accusatory finger at John. "You tell him I will never remarry. You can also tell him I plan to live to be a hundred and fifty. That man is going to be paying alimony forever."

It was a familiar refrain. To the best of John's knowledge, his father had never complained about the alimony, nor had he encouraged Leanne to remarry, which was the only condition under which the payments would end. His mother's version of the story was markedly different.

She settled onto the sofa next to him and laid her hand on his arm. "You're the one who should be thinking about marriage," she said softly.

With this example of marital bliss? No thanks! John swallowed the last of his coffee and started to rise, but his mother stopped him.

"Tell me about Fairlawn. What does your father think about your restoring his family's home?"

"He and I haven't discussed it." Or anything else.

"You know, John, your father has many flaws, but he also has connections. He could help you if you have any problems there."

Pigs would fly before John asked Henry Moreland for anything.

Two days later, John settled back in the comfortable leather seat. It might not be practical, but he was taking the Ferrari to Hidden Falls this week. The weekend had been difficult, starting with his visit to his mother on Saturday morning, and he needed—oh, how he needed—the relaxation of driving the car of his dreams.

Dreams. That was an unfortunate word choice. John didn't want to think about dreams, not when the same Technicolor vision disturbed his sleep each night. It never varied. In his dream, he was climbing the main staircase at Fairlawn, practically running in his eagerness to see the woman he knew was waiting for him at the top. He'd climb and climb, taking the stairs two at a time. His heart would pound, more with anticipation than from the effort of ascending the staircase, as he took another step and yet another. She was there. He knew it. But, no matter how long he climbed, he never reached the top. He never reached her. He'd waken, his heart still pounding, his forehead furrowed with frustration that he hadn't seen Claire.

John pressed his foot on the accelerator, then lightened the pressure. There was no point in getting a ticket. That wouldn't put an end to the dreams. He suspected nothing would. The only thing he could do was refuse to let them bother him. They were, after all, simply dreams. Although Freud might disagree, John knew that these particular dreams meant nothing. He wasn't searching for Claire. He didn't want either her or Fairlawn to be a permanent part of his life. Fairlawn was a project, nothing more, just as Claire was a business associate, nothing more. And, even if by some incredibly remote chance the dreams had some significance, John was not going to act on them. He would not. Just as he absolutely, positively was not going to take his mother's advice and consider marriage.

John forced his hands to loosen their grip on the steering wheel. He would think about pleasant things, like . . . Oh, all right. He would let himself think about Claire. Purely in a business setting, of course. The dreams and his mother's suggestions had nothing to do with the fact that he was smiling as he thought about the work awaiting him in Hidden Falls.

Renovating Fairlawn was the most exciting project John had ever undertaken. It might not be the biggest, and it certainly wasn't going to have the longest duration, but there was no doubt that he was enjoying it more than anything before. The reasons were easy to find. Of course they were. It was the fact that he was doing something new—creating a hotel rather than masterminding an urban renovation. It was also the fact that this particular property was part of his heritage. Although there were many times when John wished he were not Henry Moreland's son, he couldn't—and didn't want to—deny that he was a Moreland. Granddad's tales had instilled a deep respect for the work John's ancestors had done. Those were the reasons he looked forward to the time he spent in Hidden Falls. Claire was nothing more than the frosting on the cake, the cherry on the sundae.

It was true that he enjoyed working with her. She was a talented woman who kept him from being bored. They didn't always agree. In fact, they often disagreed. When that happened, there was no ignoring the sparks that flew between them. John enjoyed those sparks. If he were being honest, he'd admit that there were sparks even when he and Claire weren't disagreeing, and he enjoyed them too. But those sparks were caused by business, nothing more. They had nothing to do with the kiss they'd shared.

John felt his pulse race as he remembered the night in Roxanne's parking lot. He shouldn't have done it. He knew that. Kissing Claire Conners was a huge mistake. They had agreed to a business relationship. That's what she wanted. It should have been all that he wanted. He should have contented himself with a simple handshake. But he hadn't, and now he was paying the price for his foolishness.

He couldn't forget the kiss. No matter how often he told himself that he had to forget it, John failed. He thought of that kiss every time he saw Claire and far, far too many other times. And then there was the afternoon she'd stepped into his arms. Oh, she hadn't intended to. John could see how uncomfortable she was when she'd wound up so close to him.

Thank goodness she had no way of knowing how much he'd wanted to keep his arms around her or how he'd wanted to pull her even closer and kiss her again and again and again. It was ridiculous to keep thinking about that. Somehow, someway he had to stop.

"Claire's not home yet," Glinda told him an hour later when he'd parked in front of the familiar house on Maple Road. "Her cooking club is making a German meal today." Glinda opened the door fully and beckoned him inside. "Come in and keep an old woman company."

"You're not old, Glinda." It wasn't flattery. Though her roots might be gray, most days she acted younger than John's mother.

Glinda shook her head slowly. "Thank you, but the calendar says otherwise." When they reached the entry to the parlor, she stopped. "Claire left some raspberry iced tea. Would you like some?"

"No, thanks. I can only stay a few minutes. I promised I'd meet Ryan in half an hour." Which meant that there was no reason he should have come here. No reason at all. Surely he hadn't come to see Claire.

"I'm glad you stopped by." Glinda settled into her favorite wing-backed chair, her feet flat on the floor, her back as straight as ever. The woman could definitely give classes on perfect posture. John started to smile at the thought of Glinda trying to impose her standards on what he called the Slouching Generation. His smile faded as she fixed her gaze on him and said, "There's something I need to ask you."

It could be something innocuous. Perhaps she wanted his advice on replacement windows or in-line water heaters. But the look Claire's grandmother gave him told John that home renovation wasn't the subject at hand.

"You and Claire have been spending a lot of time together," she said.

He nodded. "This is one of those stages of the project that requires a lot of collaboration." Collaboration. That was a good word. Pure business.

"Indeed." If he hadn't known better, John would have said that Glinda was laughing at him. "I'm an old woman, and old women are allowed to be frank." She leaned forward slightly. "What I want to know is, what are your intentions toward my granddaughter?"

John felt the blood drain from his face. *Intentions?* "I don't understand your question. Claire and I are business associates. That's all."

This time there was no doubt about it. Glinda laughed.

John gripped the steering wheel as he drove toward the school. Somehow he'd gotten out of the house without losing any more of his composure. He recalled muttering something about needing to pick up a basketball before he met Ryan. It was a lie, of course, and John was certain that Glinda knew that. The simple fact was, he couldn't stay there and be subject to her scrutiny.

Intentions? Why had she asked him that? Though there had been no shotgun in sight, John felt as if he'd stepped into one of those old-fashioned melodramas where the heroine's father demanded that the cavalier young boy marry his daughter. Only this time, there had been no reason for marriage. He hadn't done anything more than kiss Claire.

John tightened his grip. *How had Glinda known?* John had considered the kiss a private moment, a memory he would never share with anyone else. Obviously, Claire had felt differently. She must have told her grandmother. That was the only reason John could imagine that Glinda had asked that ridiculous question.

Women! He would never understand them.

*   *   *

"You brought the Ferrari. Cool car." The kid's eyes lit with pleasure.

"Want a ride when we're done?" Just because Ryan lived only a few blocks from the school didn't mean they had to take the most direct route home.

"You bet!"

There was a spring John had never noticed in Ryan's step as he ran toward the basketball court. Perhaps today would be different. Perhaps today the boy would be able to actually get the ball through the hoop. And perhaps pigs would fly. Judging from Ryan's performance, the pigs were a better bet.

John tried not to wince as he watched the boy shoot and miss. He knew he wasn't the best of coaches, but surely if Ryan had any native talent, he'd have improved, even if only a little. But he hadn't, and John was beginning to believe that he never would. Plain and simple, basketball wasn't Ryan Francis' game.

"Have you ever considered track and field?" John asked half an hour later when they were seated in the car, cruising slowly down the streets where Ryan had told John most of his friends lived. It was, John had realized, important that the teenager be seen in the Ferrari.

Ryan turned and gave John a scornful look. "Why would I do that? Basketball's my sport."

It wasn't, but John knew better than to say that. Instead, he said mildly, "You have what my coach used to call a runner's frame. Long legs, lots of power. I think you'd be a natural at track and field."

Ryan scowled. "I'm not interested. Basketball is what I want to do. I'm gonna be a star."

In his dreams, perhaps. John was certain that the NBA would not be knocking on Ryan Francis' door anytime soon. "It's always good to have a backup plan."

The would-be basketball star gave John a glare that threatened to blister the Ferrari's paint. "You're like all the rest. You don't understand." He unfastened his seatbelt and reached for the door handle. "Let me out. I can walk home."

First elderly women, now teenagers. John was beginning to wish he hadn't come to Hidden Falls today.

"Is something wrong at Fairlawn?" Claire asked. When John had returned to the house on Maple, Glinda had been busy in her garden, leaving John and Claire alone in the kitchen where she was washing greens for a salad.

"No." Plenty of other things were wrong, but Fairlawn wasn't one of them. "Why did you ask?"

"You look upset."

"It hasn't been the best of days." And that was the understatement of the week. He wouldn't tell Claire about her grandmother's ridiculous question. He didn't want to think about that. But Claire might have some insight into Ryan's behavior.

"Ryan Francis told me I don't understand him, and he's right. That kid is the worst basketball player I've seen. It doesn't matter how much he practices, he doesn't get any better, but he won't give up. Today he told me that he's going to be a star." John ran a hand through his hair. "Why is he setting himself up for failure?"

"Because of his father."

"I thought he died a year ago."

"He did." Claire wiped her hands on a towel and turned to face John. "Ryan's father was a basketball star in high school and college. He might have gone professional, but he wanted to marry Alice, and she wasn't willing to live on the road. So, instead of being the NBA's greatest star, Mike stayed in Hidden Falls and ran the hardware store." Claire shrugged. "I don't pretend to understand a teenage boy's mind, but I imagine Ryan's trying to prove that he's his father's son."

John closed his eyes. Ryan was right. He didn't understand. After all, hadn't he spent most of his life trying not to be his father's son?

Chapter Eight

"You look happy this morning," Claire told Ruby as they settled into a comfortable jogging pace. "And it's not just the clothes." Today Ruby was wearing a new sweat suit, this one sporting a bright red stripe down the sleeves and legs. Somewhere, she had discovered matching running shoes. Though she knew she should be accustomed to it by now, it was still a mystery to Claire where her friend found so many red garments.

"I had a great night."

Claire flashed a look of mock severity at Ruby. "You had a date last night and didn't tell me. What's going on?"

"It was only Steve." A baseball cap partially shaded her face, but nothing could block the sparkle in Ruby's eyes.

"Only Steve?" Claire stared at her friend. "I thought you and he had broken up. Didn't you tell me you had incompatible world views?"

As they rounded a corner, Ruby shrugged. "That was last week. We realized none of that mattered. What mattered was that we were miserable when we were apart. So now we're back together."

Claire wished all problems were that easy to resolve. She had no illusions that she could reconcile the differences she had with John, but she did wish that she knew what was bothering him. He'd been different since his last trip to Hidden Falls. It wasn't the fact that Ryan refused to admit his limitations on the basketball court, although John claimed that was the only thing that was preying on his mind. Claire knew an evasion when she heard it. There was something else, something that was making John seem so distant.

The easy camaraderie they'd once shared that made working together so enjoyable was gone. Ever since his last trip, John had treated her like a new employee, one who was still on probation. It wasn't a pleasant situation, but Claire had no idea how to change it. Every friendly overture had been rebuffed. That was why she'd been surprised—almost shocked—when John had accepted Glinda's invitation to join them for an early Mother's Day celebration with her parents.

"I'm happy for you," Claire told Ruby. If anyone deserved happiness, it was her friend. A flock of songbirds, recently returned from their winter homes, chirped madly, as if they too were celebrating with Ruby.

"There's more." Ruby increased their pace slightly. "I'd like you to be my maid of honor."

"Wow!" Claire took a deep breath. "That was quite a date!" A week ago Ruby and Steve hadn't been speaking to each other. Now they were engaged. Claire grabbed Ruby's arm. "Stop your jogging, Ruby Baker. I need to give you a hug."

Ruby's laugh rivaled the birds' songs for pure happiness. "Please don't tell anyone else," she said as Claire hugged her. "I want to surprise everyone at school, once it's official." Ruby held out her bare left hand. "We're going shopping for a ring this afternoon."

"You're not wasting any time are you? Have you picked a date?"

Ruby nodded and named a Saturday in August. "That'll give us two weeks for a honeymoon before school starts."

"Wonderful!" Claire gave Ruby another hug. "This is the best news I've heard in weeks."

It had been a difficult week at Hidden Falls High as the last hurdle to the school consolidation was cleared. All three affected school districts had held a special referendum on the same day, and all three had approved the consolidation. All that remained was to finalize the site selection. Construction was expected to begin before the end of the summer so that the new building would be ready for students the following fall.

Claire understood the taxpayers' perspective. They'd been promised lower taxes as well as a more robust curriculum for their children. It made sense, both academically and financially. Still, it was sad to think of the school closing. An era was ending. How fortunate that Ruby was providing something happy to occupy Claire's thoughts.

"Will you go with me when I pick out my gown?" she asked.

Claire nodded. "We'll need to find a dress for me too."

Flashing a smile at Claire, Ruby started jogging again. "I hope you don't mind," she said when Claire caught up with her, "but I've already decided on the color for your dress."

"Let me guess." Claire pretended to consider the possibilities. "Could it be? Is it possible? No, you'd never choose that one." She waited until they'd crossed the street before she said. "Ruby red."

"What else?"

As Claire joined in the laughter, she felt a moment of nostalgia. So many things were changing.

Why on earth had he agreed to this? John frowned as he glanced down at the florist's box on the seat next to him. He must have been out of his mind the day he'd promised to come. He frowned again and turned left onto Maple. Three and a half blocks, and he'd be there. Three and a half blocks, and he'd be greeting Claire's parents. Why on earth had he agreed to this?

Meeting the parents was something a suitor did. John wasn't a suitor. Not now. Not in the future. No, sirree. He had no intention of being a suitor. But somehow, when Glinda had invited him to the early Mother's Day celebration that would include her son and daughter-in-law, he'd found himself nodding his head. He could tell himself that his motive had been curiosity about the people who'd been able to leave Claire behind, but that wasn't the real reason John had accepted Glinda's invitation so quickly. The real reason was that it would afford him more time with Claire. If that wasn't crazy, John wasn't sure what was. It was difficult enough maintaining a businesslike façade around her when they were at Fairlawn. How would he manage it in a purely social setting?

There was still time to turn around. He could phone Glinda, pleading an emergency at one of his other construction sites. John reached for his cell phone, then shook his head. That was the coward's way. He'd gotten himself into this pickle, and he'd get himself out.

A minute later, he was climbing the steps to the front porch.

"I'm glad you could come." Though he'd hoped Glinda would answer the door and give him a moment's reprieve, it was Claire who stood there.

John felt his heart lurch as he looked at her. Even on a bad day, Claire was more beautiful than any one woman deserved to be. Today was not a bad day. Today she was wearing a dress he'd never seen, a soft orangey colored dress—apricot, peach, some kind of fruit color—that swirled around her legs. Her arms were bare, and the top of the dress—what did they call it, a bodice?—showcased her lovely neck. She'd piled her hair on top of her head, but a couple tendrils had escaped. Though John doubted it was deliberate, it was sexy as could be. His fingers itched to brush those tendrils aside, replacing each with a kiss. But he couldn't—wouldn't—do that. Claire would be appalled. Instead, John swallowed deeply as he followed her into the house.

"Flowers." Claire smiled at the sight of the box he carried. "Glinda will be pleased."

"I hope you'll all be pleased." He placed the box on the console table and opened it. He'd chosen three wrist corsages in varying sizes. Because he hadn't known what color dresses the women would be wearing, John had insisted that the flowers be white.

"Three?"

"Your grandmother, your mother, and you." John handed Claire the smallest of the trio.

She stared at it, her blue eyes mirroring her confusion. "But I'm not a mother."

"No, you're not," he agreed. "But you are a beautiful woman, and beautiful women deserve flowers."

The color that flooded Claire's face only added to her allure. Though she was clearly embarrassed by the fact that he'd brought flowers, she slid the elastic band over her hand and sniffed the distinctive fragrances of roses and carnations.

"Thank you, John," she said softly. "They're beautiful." Then she gestured toward the living room. "Let me introduce you to my parents."

As Claire performed the introductions, John studied the middle-aged couple. Although gray now threaded the dark brown, it was clear that Claire had inherited her father's hair and eye color, while she owed her delicate bone structure to her mother.

"It's a pleasure to meet you." Those were the words his mother had taught him to use, particularly when being introduced to the older generation. In this case, John wasn't certain it would be a pleasure, but he was glad to be meeting Claire's parents. Ever since he had heard that they'd placed their careers ahead of their daughter, he'd been curious about Ken and Susan Conners, picturing them as cold and detached. They were neither, he discovered. Ken was charismatic, the kind of man John's own father would describe as being born to lead, while Susan appeared vibrantly energized and as much of a leader as her husband. Together, they would be a formidable team.

"I heard Claire is helping you restore Fairlawn," Ken Conners said when the introductions were complete and the two older women had donned their corsages.

Though the words were neutral, there was something in Ken's voice that set John's antennae quivering. Perhaps it was the way he pronounced "helping," as if Claire's contribution to the restoration were a minor one.

"Claire is a key member of the team," John said firmly. "Her eye for decorating is what will distinguish Fairlawn from its competitors. In fact, my architect calls her the secret weapon."

Susan Conners laid a hand on her husband's arm. "That's nice, isn't it Ken?" Her expression told John that Ken was the most important part of her life. "Hotels ought to have their own personalities. The ones we stay in all seem the same."

"Except for the one in Spain." Ken gave her a smile that excluded everyone else in the room, a smile designed to remind her of a shared secret.

"You're right. That one was special." Susan turned toward John. "Even with our seniority, it's hard for Ken and me to arrange layovers in the same place. We were lucky to be able to spend a week in a fabulous hotel north of Barcelona."

Glinda nodded. "I'm glad you were able to come for today."

Today? John had thought that Claire's parents were

spending the weekend in Hidden Falls. Now it appeared they were making it a day trip.

"Are you sure you want to go to Aerie?" Claire asked her parents. "I know you eat in restaurants most of the time, so I thought you might prefer a home-cooked meal. Besides, it's a fairly long ride, especially on top of all your other driving."

Ken shook his head. "There's no need for you to bother cooking, Claire. You know Mother likes gourmet food."

And what, John wanted to shout, *do you think your daughter creates?* Claire's meals were superb, rivaling or besting the finest restaurants in the country. Didn't this man know that? Didn't he care that she was trying to do something nice for them? Or was it simply what Ken had first said, that he didn't want Claire to spend time in the kitchen when their visit was so short? Since she didn't appear upset, John decided to give Claire's father the benefit of the doubt.

"Let's get this show on the road." Ken led the way to the car he and Susan had rented, insisting that he would drive. "It's part of our gift to you, Mother," he said as he ushered Glinda into the backseat.

John's initial impression of Claire's parents was reinforced on the ride to the restaurant. Both were brilliant conversationalists, their repertoire of stories seemingly limitless. With a deft sense of humor that was at times self-deprecating, Ken and Susan entertained the trio in the backseat with tales of their flights, making even lost baggage sound like an adventure. No one listening to them would doubt for a second how much they enjoyed being part of the airline industry. Surely it was only John's imagination that Claire, who'd insisted on taking the center seat, shrank a little with each anecdote.

It was his imagination, John convinced himself, for once they arrived at the restaurant Claire seemed her normal cheerful self. Oh, it was true that she didn't talk as much as normal, but neither did Glinda. Ken and Susan didn't leave much opportunity for anyone else to join the conversation. Still, the meal was enjoyable. The restaurant was one of the finest in the area, noted for its excellent steaks. And, as the name implied, the building was perched on top of a hill with breathtaking vistas.

While they were waiting for dessert to be served, Glinda turned toward her son. "I hope you'll be able to come back next year and see the changes in Hidden Falls." When Ken gave her a blank look, she continued. "By then the school will be closed, and Fairlawn will be open."

Susan smiled. "That will be good. Ken, why don't you tell everyone about the time you had that flight filled with school kids on spring break."

John felt the bile rise in his throat as once again a subject that affected Claire was dismissed. Couldn't her parents see what they were doing? No, John realized, they couldn't. Susan and Ken Conners were marvelous storytellers. John suspected they were also highly competent pilots. But parents? He'd give them a failing grade in that particular endeavor.

Poor Claire! By the time they'd returned to Hidden Falls and the elder Conners had left, John's sympathy had turned into fury. If he thought it would help, he would have told Ken and Susan Conners what a failure he considered them. If he thought it would help, he would have throttled one or both of them. But it wouldn't help. John knew that. He couldn't change Claire's parents any more than he could change his own. There was no point in even trying. All he could do was help Claire. And it was clear from the way her face tightened with strain whenever she smiled at them that Claire needed help. She might not admit it; she might not welcome it; but there was no doubt that she needed it.

"When I passed that 'Welcome to Hidden Falls' sign this morning," John said as casually as he could, "I realized that

I'd never seen the falls. Could I convince you to be my tour guide once again?"

Claire looked down at the orangey dress that had caught his eye earlier. "I'm not exactly dressed for the occasion."

She hadn't refused. John took that as a good omen. "These aren't my hiking clothes, either. I'll give you five minutes to change, and then we'll stop at Fairlawn so I can do the same."

Smiling, Claire held out her hand. "You've got yourself a deal, Mr. Moreland."

John winced, remembering the last deal they'd struck and the way a simple handshake had turned into something not so simple. Though he wanted nothing more than to gather Claire into his arms and soothe her pain, he couldn't do that. At least not here where Glinda could interrupt at any moment.

Half an hour later, he parked the car at the top of the path to the falls.

"I'm surprised there's no one else here," Claire said, surveying the empty parking lot. "This is a popular place in the summer." Today, a sunny, reasonably warm Saturday afternoon in early May should have been a good time for hikers.

"Maybe it's a little early in the day. I've heard this is a favorite evening destination for courting couples." The instant the words were out of his mouth, John regretted them. What on earth had possessed him to say that? He didn't want to think about courtship. Of course he didn't.

Claire raised an eyebrow, seemingly unaware of his consternation. "Hidden Falls is a bit short on romantic spots. Glinda said that at one time the carousel was popular, but now that that's gone, this is the best we have to offer."

As they started down the path, John failed to see its appeal to courting couples, or couples of any kind. It was barely wide enough for one person to traverse. Why did anyone come here? Surely it wasn't for the rock-strewn pathway.

The trees on both sides were pretty, but there were other trees in Hidden Falls, and they didn't require off-road travel.

The falls had better be worth the trip. It wasn't that he particularly cared about seeing water tumbling over a cliff, but John hoped that by the time they reached the falls, Claire would have relaxed. He knew that she jogged to reduce stress and hoped this walk would have similarly therapeutic effects.

"I'm surprised this isn't paved. It looks like it could be slippery." Besides being narrow, the pitch of the walkway was steeper than John had expected.

Claire, who'd been leading the way, paused, and turned toward him. "There was never enough money in the town's budget for grading or paving." She gestured toward the handrail on the river side of the path. "We're lucky we have that. Even with it, some people fall, but most of us know not to come right after a rain."

John could see the tension in her shoulders and the way she gripped the handrail. Neither, he was certain, was caused by the potentially slippery path. There had to be a way to help her relax. Perhaps this required more than physical exercise. Perhaps it was like lancing a boil to let out the poison. Since John doubted she would introduce the topic herself, he said, "I enjoyed meeting your parents." It wasn't much of an exaggeration. The initial meeting had been all right. It was only later that he'd become angry.

Claire continued walking. "Everyone likes them," she said. "They're the life of the party." Her clenched jaw told John that was small consolation.

"Claire, I . . ."

Before he could finish the sentence, she whirled around. "Let's not talk about them. Okay?"

It didn't take a genius to see that she was hurt. John didn't claim to be a genius. All he was was a man who cared. What could he do? If Claire had slipped and skinned her knee, he would know what to do. He would follow his mother's example and put a bandage on Claire's knee.

Until he'd become a teenager and too old for such attentions, Mother had also kissed the affected area, insisting that cuts and scrapes healed faster if they had a little extra love lavished on them. But this wasn't a scrape. This wound was far more difficult to heal. There were no bandages designed for this type of injury, and a kiss . . .

John stared at the beautiful young woman who walked only a foot in front of him. He wanted—oh, how he wanted!—to pull her into his arms and kiss her. But he couldn't. Not today. Today she was too vulnerable. Today she might accept the kiss as a form of healing, a psychological bandage. That wasn't the kind of kiss John wanted to give Claire. If he kissed her again, it would be because she was an attractive woman who stirred his senses. If he kissed her again, it would be because she wanted to be kissed. When he kissed her again . . . John swallowed deeply as he realized that his thoughts had changed from "if" to "when." How had that happened?

They walked in silence for a few minutes, and as they did, John heard the sound of falling water become more distinct. They must be nearing the overlook that marked the end of the path. He smelled the moisture and felt the increased humidity as spray from the falls filled the air. Though trees obscured the view of the river, John was certain that they were only yards away from the cataract that had given the town its name.

Though he felt a mild curiosity about the local landmark, John's attention was focused on the woman whose anguish was as tangible as the mist. What could he do to ease her pain?

The path curved to the right, then widened, and John found himself standing next to Claire, staring at the falls that were no longer hidden. They weren't as broad as Niagara or as tall as the ones he'd seen in the Canadian Rockies, but what they lacked in sheer size, they made up in beauty. The water tumbled over the precipice, seeming to dance when it hit the bottom of the gorge. As if that weren't enough majesty for one man to absorb, the late afternoon sunlight refracted in the mist, creating myriad rainbows.

"This is beautiful," he said softly.

Claire nodded. "I've always liked it. It's so peaceful that I used to come here whenever I needed to think."

Though John wouldn't have described the torrent as peaceful and though gazing at a waterfall wasn't the way he preferred to deal with problems, it probably explained why Claire had agreed so readily to his suggestion that they visit the falls today. "My approach is different," he told her. "I put on headphones and listen to music."

"Rock?"

John shook his head. "Beethoven." The sound of water rushing over the precipice was almost as soothing as Beethoven's Ninth Symphony.

Claire's eyes widened. "I never figured you for a Beethoven type. I prefer country, myself."

"Really?" John looked at the woman who stood next to him, trying to picture her listening to country music. Weren't all the songs about trucks, rodeos, and broken hearts?

"I shocked you, didn't I?"

"Not exactly shocked, but I am surprised. Country music doesn't seem to fit in the same picture as gourmet cooking and elegant interior design."

"Then you've got a lot to learn."

"So do you." Perhaps it was the sight of the falls. Perhaps it was the discussion of music. John wasn't sure which, and he didn't care. The result was the same. He'd thought of something that might help Claire. "Let's start next week.

There's a Philharmonic concert—Beethoven, of course. Why don't you come with me?" As Claire grimaced, John continued, "I drag my mother to it each year. She'll be glad to have someone to commiserate with."

"Misery loves company?"

"Something like that." The truth was, John hoped that meeting Leanne would show Claire that she wasn't the only one with less-than-perfect parents.

"But next weekend is Mother's Day. I don't want to intrude on your celebration."

"Was I intruding today?" When Claire shook her head, John grinned. "Turnabout is fair play."

The woman was gorgeous. Claire knew she shouldn't be surprised. After all, she had been a beauty queen. What surprised Claire was just how attractive Leanne Moreland was. The first Mrs. Moreland of her generation was a tall, slender blue-eyed blond, dressed in what had to be a designer original gown, a small fortune in sapphires draped around her neck and dangling from her ears. Though Claire had worn the royal blue dress that Glinda claimed made Claire look like a princess, next to John's oh, so elegant mother, Claire felt distinctly less than royal. She also felt out of place. The tension between John and his mother had been palpable, and—though Leanne Moreland said nothing—Claire suspected her presence was a major contributing factor.

Why had John invited her? Though Claire had doubted she'd enjoy the music, John had acted as if it was important to him that she come. Surely it wasn't to demonstrate how different their lifestyles were. Claire already knew that, and—whatever other faults he had—John wasn't a cruel man. He wouldn't deliberately humiliate her or make her feel uncomfortable. So why was Claire here in New York's premier concert hall with Mrs. Moreland and the Beautiful People?

"I must tell you again how happy I am to meet you, Claire," Mrs. Moreland said as they waited to be escorted to their seats. "For years, I've been telling John that it's time he started thinking about marriage."

Claire had heard that people's jaws dropped. She had heard that shock rendered people speechless. This was the first time she'd experienced either phenomenon. She looked around. John appeared deep in conversation with an acquaintance. Thank goodness! At least he hadn't heard that preposterous comment. "I hate to disappoint you, Mrs. Moreland," Claire said when she had recovered her composure, "but John and I are business associates. I'm helping him restore Fairlawn."

John's mother's smile left no doubt that she didn't believe Claire. "If you say so."

It was not an auspicious beginning to the evening. The few times that John had spoken of his mother, he had said she was still bitter over the divorce, even though it had been final for more than fifteen years. John hadn't told Claire that that bitterness had become corrosive, just as he hadn't told her that his mother was pushing him toward marriage, that she was as much a matchmaker as Glinda.

Or was she? When she thought about it, Claire realized that Mrs. Moreland's words to her were more like the opening salvo in a battle than a greeting to a potential daughter-in-law. Not that Claire aspired to that position. Indeed, she did not. But that didn't stop her from watching the interaction between John and his mother and becoming increasingly uncomfortable. Was this the way John had felt the day he'd spent with her parents? Claire hoped not. Mom and Dad weren't bitter. Far from it. They were happy with their careers and their marriage. It was only parenthood that didn't suit them.

"It's wonderful that you share John's love for classical

music." Though the words were addressed to her, Mrs. Moreland leaned across Claire and patted John's arm.

Before Claire could respond, John said, "Claire's tastes are eclectic."

Claire bit back a smile as she wondered how John's mother would react if she saw Claire's CD collection. It wasn't eclectic. It was pure country/western.

"Really?" Mrs. Moreland arched a perfectly plucked brow. "That's how someone once described Henry's musical preferences. It made me realize that 'eclectic' was shorthand for 'low class'." The woman didn't pull any punches where her ex-husband was concerned.

"My father preferred the Beatles to Beethoven." To Claire's surprise, there was a note of admiration in John's voice. Coming from a man who'd told her he spoke to his father no more than once a year, that seemed strange.

"Henry actually likes that vulgar song, 'Eleanor Rigby'. He used to sing it to me." There was no mistaking Mrs. Moreland's disdain. There was also no mistaking the fact that Claire was being excluded from the conversation. Even when John addressed a comment to her, his mother answered so quickly that the only way Claire could speak would be to interrupt.

For what seemed like the hundredth time, Claire asked herself why John had invited her. The comment about misery loving company didn't hold water, unless . . . Though he'd said Claire could commiserate with his mother, perhaps that was a red herring. Perhaps John had known he'd be miserable and had hoped Claire's presence would lessen it. If that was the case, Claire suspected she was failing.

"Why would anyone want to sing about lonely people?" Mrs. Moreland continued her diatribe against the Beatles' song. "Henry Moreland was never lonely a day in his life. He always had a woman on his arm. Usually a different one for each day of the week."

"Now, Mother, you know that's not true. Dad and Janet have been married for ten years."

"I never did understand what he saw in that bimbo."

Though Beethoven was not her choice of music, Claire was thankful when the conductor took his place and the concert began. At least the unpleasant conversation would end. She settled back in her seat and tried to concentrate on the music, but instead of Beethoven's sonatas, the lyrics to "Eleanor Rigby" resonated through her brain. "All the lonely people." Perhaps Henry Moreland hadn't been referring to himself. Perhaps he'd recognized that his wife was lonely, and that was the reason he'd sung that song to her. Claire thought about the comments John's mother had made and the obvious bitterness with which she laced most of her words. Was that the result of her loneliness? If so, Claire felt sorry for her, but even more she worried about the effect that bitterness had had on Leanne Moreland's son.

Claire darted another look at the man who sat next to her. Though a casual observer might believe he was intent on the music, Claire saw the tension in the way he held his head and the line of his jaw. Beethoven hadn't caused that. What could she do? When she had needed comfort, John had taken her to the falls, but there were no falls in Manhattan. Trying not to sigh, Claire forced her attention back to the music. It wasn't as bad as she'd expected, but it would never replace Waylon Jennings.

The litany of complaints that had been temporarily halted by the concert continued when the three of them dined at one of Manhattan's finest restaurants. Though the food and service were impeccable, John's mother found fault with everything. By the end of the meal, Claire's stomach was tied in so many knots that she doubted she would be able to digest what had been a series of delicious courses of food.

How did John do it? His appetite appeared unaffected by

the diatribes, and throughout the meal he tried to lighten the conversation. But each time John changed the subject, his mother found a way to complain. *Was she always this way*, Claire wondered, *or did my presence made a bad situation worse?*

It was late by the time John had taken his mother home, then headed toward the hotel where Claire was spending the night. They drove in silence, and for once the silence was not a comfortable one. Claire's thoughts roiled as she wondered what she could say or do to help John. Her own parents were not perfect—far from it—but at least she had Glinda. John, it appeared, had no one who loved him for what he was. It was no wonder he focused on his business and measured everything in terms of dollars and cents. With a role model like Leanne Moreland, it was surprising that John had not become a cynic.

When they reached the hotel and dropped Claire's suitcase in her room, John offered her a cup of coffee.

"I don't need any more caffeine," she told him, "but I could use some fresh air." Maybe, just maybe, the air would clear her head and she'd be able to find a way to salvage the evening. It was true that John was her business associate. Despite those traitorous dreams and the magical kiss they'd shared, that was the extent of their relationship. But even business associates helped each other.

As they'd walked to the elevator, Claire had seen a terrace lining the back of the hotel. Guessing that at this time of the night it would be empty, she led the way. Once outside, she breathed deeply. The air was cool and as fresh as city air could be. Claire walked to the stone railing and looked down. Subtle landscape lighting illuminated what appeared to be a formal garden. It was still too early in the year for night blooming flowers, but she smelled the sweet scent of young grass. Claire closed her eyes for a second, searching for the words that would comfort John.

Before she could speak, he touched her shoulder, turning her toward him. "I want to apologize for my mother." The crescent moon gave enough light for Claire to see the pain in his eyes. It was worse—far worse—than she'd feared. "Mother's not always that bad."

What could she say? What could she do? There had to be some way to ease that anguish. But what? Words didn't heal such deep wounds. When Claire had been hurt by her parents' absence on Christmas and her birthday, Glinda hadn't even tried to explain. She'd hugged her. Perhaps that would work. Before her courage failed, Claire threw her arms around John.

He stood immobile, as if her gesture had shocked him, and for a second Claire was afraid he'd push her away. Then, slowly, as if it were an act he had to relearn, John began to smile. "Claire, I . . ." He paused, and she saw his eyes darken. This time it wasn't pain that filled them, but something else, something sweeter yet no less powerful. "I . . ." Before she realized what he intended, John lowered his head and pressed his lips to hers.

The kiss was nothing like the first one they had shared. This one was deeper, darker, and Claire tasted desperation on his lips. Perhaps he tasted it on hers, too, for she wanted desperately to help him. Sensing how much John needed comfort, Claire returned the kiss, lacing her fingers behind his head and drawing him closer. If kisses could bring healing, she would give them freely. She would do anything to ease his pain, to show him how much she cared.

And then, gradually, the kiss changed. Claire felt the difference in John's lips. Where they had been harsh and greedy, seeking comfort, now they were soft and tender, creating pleasure. She felt the difference in his hands. Where they had gripped her tightly, as if he were afraid she would leave him, now they stroked her back, sending waves of delight through her.

This kiss had nothing to do with John's mother. It had nothing to do with giving or receiving comfort. It was a kiss between a man and a woman sharing their deepest emotions. In the space of a kiss, the world had shrunk until there was nothing in it but Claire and John. Oh, how she hoped it would never end!

Chapter Nine

"Claire, you're just the person I wanted to see."

Claire dropped the Brussels sprout into the bag before she turned to smile at Alice Francis. Though they'd spoken on the phone several times, it had been months since Claire had seen Ryan's mother. Today the small supermarket's produce aisle was more crowded than normal, serving as an impromptu meeting place as well as a source of fresh vegetables.

"I can't thank you enough for introducing Ryan to John Moreland," Alice continued, her face glowing with pleasure. "It's made such a difference. My son needed a role model, and John has been that. Ryan comes home from practice raving about him." She stepped aside, allowing two other women better access to the carrots. "Of course, that red car doesn't hurt. Ryan informed me that when he gets his first job, he's going to buy a Ferrari just like that." Alice's lips twisted in an ironic smile. "I didn't have the heart to tell him that he'll be working for a long, long time before he can afford one of those."

If ever. But Claire didn't say that. Instead, she nodded slowly, thinking of the changes she'd seen in Ryan since he and John started playing basketball together. The lackluster academic performance she'd noted all year was gone. Now Ryan was attentive and no longer seemed reluctant to volunteer answers.

"A boy needs his dreams," Alice said, "and John Moreland helped my son find his again. He's a good man."

"Yes, he is."

He was also much more than that, Claire reflected as she stood in line at the checkout counter. She could tell herself he was a business associate. She could claim he was a friend. Both of those were true, but John was more.

Claire bagged her groceries and headed toward her car. It was warmer than usual for late May. The lilacs had started to bloom, leaving no doubt that spring was in its full glory. Spring. Glinda claimed the season made a young man's thoughts turn to love. Perhaps it wasn't only men who were affected. Perhaps the season was the reason why Claire couldn't stop thinking about it.

As she loaded the bags into the back of her SUV, Claire remembered the times she and Glinda had talked about love.

"You'll know it when it finds you," her grandmother had promised. "When you love someone, he's the most important thing in your life." At the time, Claire had thought she loved Randy, the high school senior who'd been the subject of every girl's dreams. "Don't be fooled," Glinda had continued. "Love is about giving, not taking."

At the time, Claire hadn't understood. She did now. And that was how she knew that John wasn't simply a business associate or a friend. He was the man she loved. It wasn't only that she continued to dream of him, although dreams of a life together were a nightly occurrence. Claire might have been able to dismiss the dreams, but the fact was, thoughts of John occupied her waking hours, too. She'd be at school, showing a student how to cream butter and sugar, and she'd picture herself making cookies for John and their children. She'd be jogging with Ruby, and she'd imagine John joining her, stopping in a secluded area for a kiss.

A kiss. If she had had any doubts about the depth of her feelings for John Moreland, they vanished that night at the concert. That was when she'd realized how deeply she cared for him. She'd felt his pain as if it were her own, and more than anything, she'd wanted to comfort him, to somehow assuage his pain. She'd seen his loveless life and had wanted to change it. She wanted—oh! how she wanted—to give John love.

And then there was the kiss they'd shared on the terrace. The feelings that kiss aroused told Claire more clearly than any dream could that she loved John with all her heart. Being in his arms, kissing him, and having that kiss returned, had been more wonderful than Claire had thought possible. If dreams and wishes could come true, she would marry John and they'd live happily ever after. If dreams and wishes could come true, her love would be enough to heal his wounds. But dreams and wishes didn't always come true, and Claire knew it was likely these would not. It took two to make a marriage and to create a life of happily ever after. She was ready, but John was not. Sadly, he probably never would be.

Claire started the engine and headed home. John had said that he was not a marrying man. Now she knew why. Though he might be serving as a role model for Ryan Francis, John himself had no role model. At least not a positive one. Seeing the results of his parents' bitter divorce, it was no wonder that he had no intention of even considering matrimony. With a similar example, Claire would have been just as wary. She, too, would have thought that stories of wedded bliss were nothing more than fairy tales. But they weren't. Glinda was proof of that. So, too, in their own way, were her parents. Though they were not typical, or even ideal parents, no one could doubt the happiness of their marriage. John had no such experiences, and that meant that what was a dream to Claire would be a nightmare for him.

"Ms. Conners." It was the next morning, and Claire was in her first class. She turned to the student, chagrined that her thoughts had been wandering . . . toward John, of course.

"Yes, Heather?"

"Do you know anything more about the new school?"

It was the question everyone asked themselves, at least once a day. "No more than you, I'm afraid."

"Michael's father said the mayor tried to convince them to build on that big farm outside of town, but they refused," Kathy Winick told the class.

Heather wrinkled her nose. "My mom says it's all political."

Claire couldn't refute that. "Many decisions are."

"That doesn't make it right." Though it was Kathy who made the protest, the others nodded in agreement. Claire wished she could offer them reassurances, but she wouldn't lie. The truth was, she was just as distressed by the situation as they were.

"Is it true that you won't be teaching after next year?" Heather asked.

Claire nodded, a little surprised that the students didn't know about the Town Council's decree that she serve as Fairlawn's general manager. "I've agreed to manage Fairlawn."

"I thought that was part-time."

Claire shook her head. "I need to be there every day." It wasn't an exaggeration. Claire knew that, since she wouldn't have an assistant, she'd be on call 24/7.

"Bummer."

Kathy nodded. "Double bummer. We'll miss you. You make it easy to learn."

The bubble of happiness that welled up inside her surprised Claire by its intensity. While it was true that she would earn more money managing Fairlawn than she did teaching, how could you put a price tag on the fact that she'd helped students? "I enjoy teaching," she told her class. "And you guys make it fun." More fun than she'd dreamed possible. The work on Fairlawn was exhilarating, but for the first time, Claire realized how much she'd miss teaching. If only she could do both! But that, Claire knew, was impossible. If she tried, she wouldn't be able to do justice to either one.

"Do you mind if we go an extra mile?" Ruby asked when they met for their Saturday morning jog. "I'm worried about fitting into my gown." The wedding dress Ruby had selected was a slender column of satin designed for a well-toned body.

Though Claire suspected that Ruby would be too busy with wedding plans to gain an ounce in the next three months, she nodded. Perhaps the additional exercise would reduce her own stress levels. They'd been on red alert all week. "Sure," she agreed. "Let's go down to the river and back."

They chatted casually as they ran down Falls, turning right onto Mill to complete their loop. As they jogged past the five-story brick building that dominated the river's edge, Ruby slowed her pace a little, then inclined her head toward the abandoned mill.

"It sure will be strange when it's gone."

"What do you mean?"

"Steve says there's a serious buyer. He doesn't know who it is, but if the deal goes through, the plan is to tear down the mill and build condos." Ruby jogged in place, as if visualizing modern condominiums in the place of the old mill.

Frowning, Claire considered the possibilities. She could understand why a developer would be interested. The location was picturesque, and if the trees along the river were cut down, residents would have a view of the falls. Would Hidden Falls change its name if that happened? Claire's

frown deepened. This discussion was doing nothing to reduce her stress levels. "More change," she muttered. "And
not necessarily a good one." The Moreland Mills building
was a landmark, an important part of Hidden Falls' past.
While many considered it a white elephant, as she'd once
told John, Claire felt an almost inexplicable connection to
the old factory.

"Times change, Claire." Ruby increased her pace. "A century ago," she said between deep breaths, "the mill was pros-
pering. Now it's an empty building." She turned right onto
Bridge, heading away from the river bank. "It's like that old
carousel. It was dismantled because people wanted more exciting rides than a merry-go-round."

Claire glanced at the park where the carousel had once
stood. Although it had formerly been a hub of the town's activities, now there was little more than weeds and litter on
the grounds. "Glinda told me that people used to ride the
carousel when they were courting." *Courting!* What a poor
choice of words. When she saw Ruby's eyes light with curiosity, Claire quickly changed the subject.

Unfortunately, though it was easy enough to distract Ruby
with a discussion of the hors d'oeuvre selection for her wedding reception, it was not so easy to stop thinking about the
mill. Visions of the historic building being razed and replaced by condos flitted through Claire's mind as she show-
ered and dressed for her meeting with John and Rick. There
was no doubt that having people living on Mill Street was
preferable to having empty blocks, but other than a modest
increase in tax revenues, Claire wasn't convinced that condos would have any long-term effect on the town. Hidden
Falls needed more than a few new houses. It needed something that would attract business. But what?

She was still pondering the question as she climbed into
her SUV for the short drive to Fairlawn. It was unlikely that

a company would want to open a manufacturing plant on the site of the old mill. Though it had been a large factory when it was constructed, by twenty-first century standards, it was woefully undersized. Besides, the railroad that had once transported the finished textiles to markets in New York and Philadelphia was now defunct.

Claire accepted the fact that there was little possibility Hidden Falls could attract a manufacturing company. But what about a company that provided services rather than hard goods? Consumer hot lines, hotel and airline reservations, payroll and accounts receivable. Claire shook her head as she thought of how many of those services had been outsourced over the past decade. Hidden Falls couldn't compete with countries like India and China. Though manufacturing and back office services were out, surely there was another answer. If there was, Claire hadn't found it by the time she reached Fairlawn.

As she pulled into the long drive, Claire felt a familiar surge of excitement. How she loved this old building, and how fortunate she was to be part of its renovation! The Fairlawn project would have been a wonderful one even without John, but the fact that it was his idea and his ancestral home made it extra special.

Claire took a deep breath, savoring the fresh air as she climbed out and looked for the man she loved. He was nowhere in sight. Instead of a tall, handsome blond man striding purposefully around his estate, Claire saw Rick and Josh sitting quietly on the front steps. The scene was so peaceful that it could have been a Norman Rockwell painting, if the artist ignored Josh's grip on the small wooden carousel horse. Without asking, Claire knew that nothing had changed. The boy was still locked in his private nightmare, unable to speak and refusing to let the painted pony out of his sight.

"Hello, beautiful lady!" Rick accompanied his words with a wolf whistle that made Claire smile. Had another man whistled, she might have found it offensive, but she knew this was nothing more than Rick's way of teasing her and—more importantly—a way of entertaining his son. John had confided that the doctors had advised Rick to be as verbal as possible around Josh, in the hope that he would emulate the sounds and speak again.

"I trust you have some of your raspberry tea in that jug." Though his words were directed at Claire, Rick tousled the boy's hair.

"It just so happens that I do." Claire settled herself on the front step next to Josh and pulled a large Thermos and four unbreakable glasses from her bag. "Would you like some?"

The boy nodded, carefully transferring the carousel horse to his left hand so that he could hold the glass in his right. As they drank, Rick gave Claire a quick recap of the week's activities. Though she tried to listen, Claire found her attention veering between Hidden Falls and Josh. A dying town and a traumatized child had nothing in common other than the fact that Claire wished with all her heart that she could find a way to cure them.

"Is something wrong?"

The directness of Rick's question startled her. "No. Yes. I don't know."

"That just about covers the gamut." Claire turned, surprised that she hadn't heard John's approach. He stood at the side of the porch, his smile betraying more than a hint of amusement. "So, which one is it?"

She shrugged. "A little of all of them, I guess. You know I'm worried about the town and what the closing of the school will mean for us. Today I heard that the mill is being sold. The buyer's going to tear it down and build condos." John's expression told Claire that he was not the buyer. For a brief moment, she had entertained the hope that he'd decided to invest in Hidden Falls after all. But it was clear that he had not changed his mind. "It's taking me a while to get used to the idea of not seeing the mill. And then," she added softly, "I realized that I'll miss teaching."

John nodded slowly. "You can always back out of Fairlawn. I won't hold you to the contract. We all know that working here wasn't your idea."

But if she left, there would be no Fairlawn. Apparently fearing that either she or John might renege on their agreement, the Town Council had given only provisional approval to the project. Unless Claire and John worked together, that approval would be rescinded.

"I wouldn't do that," she said. "This is exciting. It's what I've always dreamed of doing. It's just . . ."

Rick gave her a sympathetic look. "Choices aren't always easy." He tousled Josh's hair again, the gesture reminding Claire of the lucrative contracts he had turned down, because they would have required him to leave Josh alone too often. Her own concerns paled when compared to Rick's. There she was, feeling sorry for herself that her life wasn't perfect, that she would never have a happily-ever-after with John, that she'd had to choose between teaching and running a hotel. How selfish she'd been! Her life might not be perfect, but it was pretty close, especially when she considered Rick's. In one afternoon, he'd lost his wife and part of his son.

Claire knew that being a single parent was a challenge. Being a single parent of a troubled child had to be almost unbelievably difficult, and yet she'd never heard Rick complain. Though she might be a teacher, she could take lessons from him.

Oblivious to her thoughts, Rick pulled out his blueprint case and unrolled the sheets. "I worked on the changes you suggested," he told Claire, "but you'd better check that I got them all."

The rest of the afternoon was pure business, and somehow Claire managed to concentrate on it. It was easier when Rick was there. Somehow, having him and Josh nearby helped defuse the tension that seemed to build each time she was with John. It wasn't anything John said or did. It was simply the fact that he was in the same room that made her pulse race and seemed to sensitize every one of her nerve endings. When they were together, Claire felt more energized, more aware of her surroundings, more alive than she did when they were apart. That was good, because it helped with the project. But it was also bad, because it made her dream dreams that would never come true.

"Well, sport, ready to go?" Rick smiled at his son as he rolled the blueprints.

Josh nodded and scampered toward their SUV. Claire followed more sedately, preparing for their end-of-day ritual. Ever since their first meeting, Claire had brought a special treat for the boy. She'd keep it hidden inside her bag, waiting to pull it out after he was settled for the ride home, his seat belt fastened, the carousel horse resting in his lap. Only then would Claire hand him the cookie or cake she'd made for him. Rick had told her that Josh seemed to enjoy the fact that the treat was his alone, that Rick wasn't included.

Today Josh gave her his usual shy smile, then turned his attention back to the carousel horse. A stargazer, its head was tilted upward, its mane gilded as many of the more elaborate painted ponies' were. It was without a doubt a beautiful horse, which was probably the reason Josh's mother had treasured it.

Claire looked at the small statue again, noticing not just the way Josh stroked the mane but also the way his whole body seemed to relax when he stared at the horse. Merry-go-rounds, Glinda had told Claire, had therapeutic effects. It was Glinda's assertion that no one could be unhappy around a carousel. That was why people would travel long distances to ride one, or even to stand on the sidelines, watching the painted ponies revolve while the Wurlitzer organ poured out its music, beckoning others to come close. Carousels, Glinda claimed, were magic.

As she waved farewell to Rick and Josh, Claire's mind whirled faster than a merry-go-round. Could that be the answer? She turned to John, holding up her bag. "I think there's another glass or two of tea left. Would you like some?"

He raised an eyebrow. "Am I in trouble?"

"No." That wasn't the response she'd expected. "Why did you think you were?"

"Because you're wearing that 'I need to talk to John' look."

Claire busied herself pouring the tea, trying to ignore the fact that John could read her thoughts so easily. "I do want to talk to you," she admitted. When they were once more sitting on the steps, she continued. "You know I'm worried about the town."

"You have mentioned that a time or two." John didn't bother to hide his sarcasm. He was serious, though, as he said, "I wish there were something I could do about the school closing, but there isn't. You know that."

"It wasn't the school I was thinking about today. I keep trying to find something that will bring business to Hidden Falls."

John shook his head. "I don't mean to be cruel, but other than Fairlawn, the town doesn't have much to offer. Even Fairlawn is a risk."

Claire raised an eyebrow. This was the first time John had spoken of risks.

"I know it won't be a destination for week-long vacations," he continued. "There's simply not enough to do in the area. But I'm betting that Fairlawn will be ideal for weekends and mini vacations."

Claire's spirits lifted. John's concerns were the perfect segue to her proposal. "Seeing Josh gave me an idea." If John agreed, it could help him as well as Hidden Falls. "Glinda keeps telling me that antique carousels have become a big drawing card. People are so excited about them that they'll come from hundreds, sometimes thousands, of miles away to see one. They even have a name for their enthusiasm. They call it carousel fever."

John drained the last of the tea, then set the glass on the porch. If he was interested in her story, he gave no hint of it.

"The carousel we had here was unique," Claire continued. "It was the very first Ludlow carousel ever made." Rob Ludlow, who'd married one of the Moreland daughters, had been a famous carousel carver a century earlier. The combination of his distinctive style and the small number of carousels he'd created made the individual animals highly desirable to collectors.

John stared into the distance. "That may be true, but the merry-go-round is gone."

This conversation was not going the way Claire had hoped. It was clear that John had not caught a case of carousel fever. "Glinda says the animals aren't very far away. She remembers when the carousel was dismantled and the parts were auctioned off. According to her, locals bought the horses."

"I don't know much about it, but I've heard that restoration is very expensive."

"It is." Though Claire wasn't sure of the exact figures, she knew that restoring the Hidden Falls merry-go-round would cost tens of thousands of dollars. "That's why I wondered if you'd consider making the carousel part of the Fairlawn project. It would be something your guests would enjoy. It would give them another reason to extend their visits."

"No."

Claire stared at him, surprised by the curt reply. "They would enjoy it, John. It would be like the period costume balls you're planning."

He kept his eyes fixed on the distance. "I'm not disputing that. The guests might enjoy looking at a carousel. They might even want to ride it. The 'no' relates to the money involved. JBM Enterprises will not finance anything else in Hidden Falls."

"But . . ."

"Ever since I set foot in this town, people have been trying to find ways to use me. They seem to think that just because my name is Moreland, I feel deep ties to this place. They seem to think that I have equally deep pockets and that I'll be willing to empty them for anything remotely connected to the Moreland name. They're wrong. I won't."

"But . . ."

"There are no 'buts,' Claire. The answer is no."

It was inexcusable. Though he hadn't meant to, he had hurt her. John stomped up the stairs, as if the extra energy he was exerting would help clear his foul mood. There was nothing wrong with refusing to be an open checkbook, he told himself as he yanked a dresser drawer. Unlike Claire, he didn't feel a need to save this rundown town. He had every right to choose his own projects, every right to say "no" when someone presented one as preposterous as restoring an old children's ride.

John clenched his jaw, trying to defuse the tension that had radiated through his body, making his neck more rigid than a steel I beam. There had been no need to snarl at Claire. Restoring the carousel wasn't a bad idea, if you believed that Hidden Falls should be restored. An antique merry-go-round would provide a focal point for the downtown area, if that downtown area were being revitalized. But it wasn't, at least not by John Moreland.

Be that as it may, he shouldn't have been so abrupt. What he'd said hadn't been wrong, but he could have found a better way to say it. The truth was, John wasn't angry with Claire; he was angry with himself.

He glared at the shirts. Not one of them looked suitable for dinner with Claire and Glinda. He shoved the drawer closed, clenching his jaw again. The problem wasn't just the carousel; it was the whole project. From the very beginning, this had been different from anything John had worked on. That should have been his clue to get out. But he hadn't, and look where that had gotten him. Every time he turned around, there was something new, something drawing him closer to the town. John didn't like that any more than he liked the fact that the project had made him question his whole life. He wanted answers, not questions.

His life had been on an even keel before he'd come to Hidden Falls, and look at it now. He was spending time he couldn't afford playing basketball with a teenager whose skills were charitably described as "minimal." He was spending still more time that he couldn't afford worrying about the town. John hadn't been lying when he'd told Claire he wished he could save the school, but he couldn't. That wasn't a situation that could be fixed by throwing money at it.

John worried about Ryan Francis; he worried about the school; he worried about the town, and all that worrying worried him. Why was this happening? He'd never felt like this before.

Then there was Claire. The lovely Claire. TLC. John took a deep breath. What an idiot he was! He knew better. Indeed, he did. He knew how foolish he was, and yet he couldn't stop thinking about her. No matter what he did, no matter where he went, he thought of Claire. The dreams that disturbed his sleep each night were bad enough, but the days were worse. Everything reminded him of Claire. He'd see a roll of blueprints and remember how a lock of her hair had tumbled into her face when she'd been studying one and how badly he'd wanted to tuck that tendril behind her ear. He'd be sitting at home, surfing the channels, and an ad for some restaurant would pop up. Though the food bore no resemblance to anything she had served, it would remind him of the delicious meals they'd shared, and he'd wish he were sitting across the table from Claire, savoring her company as well as her food.

John stared at the dresser. What had he been looking for? His hands formed into fists as he realized how often he had this problem, how often thoughts of Claire would make him forget what he was supposed to be doing.

He could endure the casual memories. They weren't the worst. The worst was, whenever he saw a couple together, he'd remember the kisses he and Claire had shared. The first kiss had been wonderful, but it was nothing, nothing at all, compared to the second. John couldn't forget how it had felt to hold Claire in his arms, how sweet her lips had been, and how he hadn't want to let her go. Ever. And those thoughts would lead inevitably and inexorably to thoughts he didn't want to entertain, thoughts of gold bands, solemn promises, and happily-ever-after.

Was that love? Rick claimed that it was. He claimed that John was in love with Claire. But he wasn't. He couldn't be. After all, how could you be in love when you weren't sure that any such thing existed? Love was a fantasy, a marketing device that the jewelers and florists of America had invented to sell their products. It wasn't real, any more than Santa Claus and the Tooth Fairy were real. It was nothing more than a myth, an urban legend.

John shook his head as he opened the drawer again and

grabbed the first shirt his hand touched. That wasn't true. Love did exist. Rick had loved Heidi. Others loved, even if their happily-ever-after didn't last forever. But Morelands? It appeared that they lacked the proper DNA to love. Look at Dad. He was on wife number three, and if Mother was to be believed, the only reason he hadn't divorced Janet was that he couldn't afford any more alimony. Then there was Mother herself. She'd been so badly damaged by the divorce that she'd turned into a bitter woman. So much for Morelands and love.

John turned on the shower and waited for the water to warm. He wasn't sure what it was that he felt for Claire, but he was sure of one thing. He could not risk hurting Claire the way his father had hurt his mother. Call it love, call it loyalty, call it simple human compassion. He would not do anything to injure Claire. She'd already been hurt by her parents. John wouldn't inflict any more pain on her. No matter how often he dreamed about weddings and happily-ever-after, he had to back away. Where love and marriage were concerned, Morelands were a bad risk.

He stepped into the shower, quickly lathering his hair. As the soap drained, John managed a wry smile. If only he could wash away his problems as easily as he had the day's dust. If only he could let his memories of Claire and his dreams of a future with her go down the drain. But he couldn't. Each time that he was with Claire, the feelings grew stronger. That was why he couldn't stay here. It would be impossible to maintain a purely business relationship once school ended and they were working side-by-side six days a week. There were many things John could do, but that was not one of them.

Grabbing a towel, he tried to clear his thoughts and find a solution to the dilemma. John frowned as he realized there was only one answer. He had to abandon the project. *That wasn't the coward's way,* he told himself. It was the prudent businessman's way of cutting his losses. It was also the best—perhaps the only—solution for him and Claire. He would be away from Claire and the distracting, disturbing thoughts that plagued him when they were together. It would be better for both him and Claire. She could continue teaching. John knew she hadn't resigned her position, so the change of plans wouldn't leave her without a job. Besides, hadn't she said that she knew she'd miss her classes? This was the answer, the only answer. The one way John could get his life back on track was to build a life without Claire.

Why, oh why, did that life seem so bleak?

Chapter Ten

He wasn't a coward. John turned the key and put the car into drive. It wasn't cowardly to phone Claire rather than give her the news in person. And could he help it if he got voice mail instead of a person? John winced slightly as he turned onto Bridge Street. The fact was, he'd been relieved when he'd heard the fourth ring and realized that voice mail would pick up the call. He hoped that relief didn't show in his voice when he told her that he had to return to New Jersey and that he'd call on Monday with more information. By then, John hoped fervently, he would have concocted a plausible story for why he was halting the Fairlawn project. Though he'd try to include at least a grain of truth, the story would not make even the slightest reference to his feelings and his fears. John Moreland's shortcomings were not subject to any full disclosure rules.

He glanced down, frowning when he saw his loafers. Another thing he'd forgotten. John wasn't supposed to be wearing loafers any more than he was supposed to be in the car, heading toward the highway. He was supposed to be shooting baskets with Ryan. Turning the steering wheel to the left,

John executed a quick U-turn. Even if he wasn't dressed for a basketball court, he couldn't abandon the teenager without an explanation. That would be truly cowardly, and John Moreland wasn't a coward. Was he?

"John!" A grin lit Ryan's face as John pulled close to the curb. "You're late, man."

"Sorry." It was almost a reflex action, muttering the word, but the odd feeling deep inside him made John realize that he meant it. He was sorry, not simply that he was late for practice with Ryan, but—more importantly—he regretted the fact that he might never see the boy again. "I need to go back to New Jersey to resolve a problem." It wasn't really a lie. There was a problem, a huge problem, and John hoped that he'd be able to resolve it at the condo. At home, he corrected himself. At home. The condo was his home, not Fairlawn.

Ryan looked at John's neatly pressed slacks and loafers. "No big deal." The expression on his face said the opposite.

"I can't play, but there's nothing stopping me from coaching. Let's see what you can do."

Ryan grinned and sprinted toward the basketball court. He tried. There was no doubt that the boy was trying, but no matter how skillfully he dribbled, when the ball left his hand, it did not fall through the hoop. Most times it didn't even come close to hitting the backboard. Ryan was worse than ever. The little progress that John had seen over the past few weeks had evaporated, or perhaps he had only imagined it. Perhaps the teenager had always been this bad. Each time Ryan tossed the ball over his head, John wanted to close his eyes rather than watch Ryan's hopeful expression, followed by a palpable disappointment when he flubbed the shot.

It was probably only ten minutes, but it felt like an hour later when Ryan dribbled the ball toward John, a grin on his face. "I'm getting better," he announced. "I can feel it." When John did not reply, the teenager continued. "You see it, don't you?"

"No, Ryan, I don't." John tried to soften the blow. "What I see is you trying really hard, but I don't see the improvement." He laid a hand on Ryan's shoulder. "I think you need to face the fact that you'll never be a basketball star. You should channel your energy in a different direction—maybe track and field."

Ryan's face reddened. "You're wrong. All wrong." He ducked, dislodging John's hand, then glared at him. "I'll show you." Before John knew what the boy intended, he headed for the other side of the field, running with a speed that would qualify him for the track team.

"Come back!"

"No!" Ryan shouted the word over his shoulder. "I don't ever want to see you again. I thought you were my friend, but you aren't."

He had certainly made a mess of that, John reflected as he climbed back into the Ferrari. He should have realized that Ryan wasn't ready to hear the truth. He should have left him with his dreams. John sighed. It seemed that marriage wasn't the only thing he wasn't cut out for. Where basic human relations were concerned, John Moreland was as much a failure as Ryan was at basketball. What a sorry state of events.

"He's not coming back." Claire stared at the contents of the crisper, trying to decide whether to slice celery or shred carrots for the salad. It wasn't a life altering choice, but in her current frame of mind, making the perfect tossed salad ranked right up there with achieving world peace. If she could accomplish the first, could the second be far behind?

"What makes you think that? He said he'd call again on Monday." Glinda sat at the kitchen table, a glass of iced tea in front of her.

"I know John. I can tell when he's lying." Claire pulled both the celery and the carrots out of the crisper, then gave the refrigerator door a push. The soft thump as it swung closed was somehow satisfying. "There is no emergency. John's just using that as an excuse."

"Do you really think he'll abandon Fairlawn?" Glinda asked, her voice filled with doubt. Like the original Glinda, Claire's grandmother was a perennial optimist.

Claire turned, leaning against the counter. "I do." Wrong words. They conjured images that would never turn into reality, images of white gowns and wedding vows. "John was different today," Claire told her grandmother. "He kept his distance, almost as if he didn't want to be in the same room. Even when he was disagreeing with me, he wouldn't make eye contact." How it hurt to admit that.

Glinda sipped her tea, the furrows in her forehead telling Claire she was weighing her words. "John must have been having a bad day. We all do, occasionally."

If only the explanation were that simple. "He was fine with Rick and Josh. It was just me." To Claire's chagrin, her voice cracked.

Glinda pushed a chair away from the table. "Sit down, Claire. This is not a conversation to be undertaken standing up."

"But dinner . . ."

"Can wait. Sit down."

As soon as Claire was settled, Glinda took her hand between both of hers. It was a gesture she'd repeated countless times over the years whenever she had thought that Claire needed comfort. "I don't want to pry into your personal life," Glinda said softly, "but did something happen between you and John?"

Besides two wonderful kisses? Claire wouldn't tell anyone, not even Glinda, about them. "The only thing different about today was that I asked him to consider financing a restoration of the old carousel."

"That's a great idea."

Claire shook her head. "John didn't think so. He made it very clear that he wouldn't spend another penny in Hidden Falls. The refusal was bad enough, but I think it was my suggestion that made him reconsider the whole Fairlawn project."

Glinda sat silently for a moment, stroking Claire's hand. Today her touch brought no comfort. "What are you worried about?" she asked at last. "You have a five-year contract, regardless of what happens."

"I wouldn't take the money if I wasn't working at Fairlawn. It wouldn't be fair."

"I see." Glinda nodded.

Though the words should have been noncommittal, Claire felt her grandmother's disappointment. It made no sense. "Do you think I should be paid for doing nothing?"

"I didn't say that, and no, I don't." Glinda's eyes were serious as she looked at Claire. "What I see is that you're at a crossroads. You need to make some decisions about what's important in your life and what you want the future to hold."

She made it sound so simple. It wasn't. "I don't control the future."

"Not everything, but probably more than you realize." Glinda stared at the poster of the original Glinda, as if seeking inspiration. "Tell me, Claire. Do you love John?"

Claire swallowed deeply. It was one thing to admit it to herself, quite another to speak the words aloud. "Yes," she said in little more than a whisper.

Glinda's eyes sparkled as she clapped her hands in delight. "I knew it! I knew from the first time I met him that John was the man for you!"

Claire shook her head. "It's not that simple. John and I are very different people. Just because I love him doesn't mean that he loves me or that we have a future together."

"You can create your future, Claire. I'm confident of that." Glinda's voice was serious as she continued. "Of course, it'll mean doing something that's difficult for you."

"And what is that?"

"You need to take risks."

What was her grandmother talking about? "I do take risks."

Glinda raised both brows. "Do you? I'm talking about big things. Think about it, Claire. When was the last time you let yourself risk failure?"

Two hours later, when she'd cooked dinner and washed the dishes, Claire was still asking herself that question. Glinda had retired to the parlor, a book in hand, and following an impulse she couldn't explain, Claire had climbed the stairs to the attic. Now she was sitting in the suite she'd decorated, the suite that John had once occupied, trying to answer her grandmother's question.

When had she risked failure? Claire ran her hand over the lemon yellow upholstery. The truth was, she couldn't remember. When she had finished college, she could have moved anywhere. She hadn't. Was that because she feared risk? It was true there had been no risk in returning to Hidden Falls and living with Glinda. That had been easy.

What about her career choice? She had a degree in hotel administration and could have pursued that field. Instead, Claire had decided on education. At the time, the supply of FCS teachers had been far less than the demand, meaning that there had been virtually no risk in choosing teaching as a career. Was Glinda right? Was Claire afraid of risk?

She rose and walked to the window, drawing the drapes closed. The evidence certainly appeared overwhelming. In retrospect, it was obvious that Claire wanted guarantees. Teaching, once you received tenure, was pretty much guaranteed. Or at least it had been until this year. Living with

Glinda provided Claire with a home devoid of risks. She could live in this house for the rest of her life. Yes, she sought guarantees. That was why she had insisted on the five-year contract with John. Claire hadn't been willing to shoulder the risk of being unemployed. Glinda was right about that.

Was she also right that Claire could create her own future, that she could make her dreams come true? Claire gripped the chair arms so tightly that her knuckles whitened. It would be wonderful it that were the case, but she wasn't certain it was. After all, Claire's dream of the future didn't involve only herself.

When she thought about what she wanted the future to hold, Claire was reminded of one of the towels that Moreland Mills had created almost a century ago. Though the weave was deceptively simple, the combination of different colored yarns resulted in a pattern that rivaled a French tapestry in its complexity. Ordinary cotton had been turned into something extraordinary. If she could make her dreams come true, the future would be equally extraordinary. What Claire wanted was a life with John, a life as his wife, his partner, his best friend and—if they were so blessed—the mother of his children. Simple and yet complex. Ordinary and yet extraordinary. That was her dream.

Claire walked around the room, touching the furniture that she'd chosen so carefully. The room was as close to perfect as she could make it. Creating it had been more than a class assignment; it had been the realization of a dream. Admittedly, it was small dream, compared to the one of love, marriage, and happily-ever-after with John, but Claire had made it come true. Could she do that again?

She stroked the bedspread, remembering the hours she had spent tailoring it. When she'd been decorating the room, she'd spent literally months of her life making certain that everything was done perfectly. All that effort had been necessary to turn a dream into reality. She'd worked tirelessly on the room. What had she done to create a future with John? Wincing, Claire answered her question. Nothing.

She closed her eyes as she pictured John's face this afternoon. Though he'd done his best to appear stoic, Claire had seen the pain and confusion in his eyes. He'd told her that he felt as if he were being exploited, and she'd done nothing to contradict that belief. She could have told John how important he was to her, that she'd thought of the carousel restoration as another project that they could work on together, but she hadn't. She could have explained that being with him was more important than the economic benefits to Hidden Falls, but she hadn't. She could have told him that she loved him and wanted to share his life, but she hadn't.

The reason was easy to find. Taking any one of those actions involved risks. Lots of them. There was the risk that a life with John would require Claire to leave Hidden Falls. She was comfortable here. Moving to a new place would mean making new friends, possibly being rejected by some people. How would she handle that?

Claire's vision of the future included children. It didn't take Freud to tell her that was the reason she dreamed of the nursery almost every night. But there was the risk that John might not want children. It was clear that he hadn't had positive role models for parenthood. Perhaps he wouldn't be willing to take the risk of being a less-than-perfect father. Could Claire be happy without children? She wasn't sure.

And then there was the biggest risk of all. John might not love her. If she confessed her feelings, he might tell her that he didn't care, that he thought of her as nothing more than a business associate or at best a friend. What would she do then? Her dream would be shattered beyond repair.

Claire began to pace the floor. There were risks, huge risks,

if she told John of her love. There were no risks if she did
nothing, but there was also no reward. The question was, was
she willing to give up the possibility of happiness to avoid
risking rejection? Everything she'd done so far said "yes."

Back and forth. Back and forth. As her feet moved me-
thodically, Claire's mind continued to whirl. She'd been
willing to fight for Hidden Falls. That was why she'd asked
the Town Council to attach strings to John's zoning variance.
That was why she wanted to restore the carousel. If she'd
fight for a town, why wasn't she willing to fight for her own
happiness? Claire touched the wall, then turned, admitting
the truth. She had been afraid. She was still afraid.

Glinda was right. Claire feared the unknown and was willing to settle for second best rather than face failure or rejection. Could she change? Glinda was also right when she said
change would be difficult for Claire. It would take courage
to tell John she loved him. Despite the wonderful kisses
they'd shared, she didn't know how he felt about her. It was
one thing to kiss a woman, another to pledge your life to her.
What if John didn't love her? Though Claire knew he would
not laugh at her, if John's face filled with pity as he told her
that he did not return her feelings, something inside Claire
would die. She knew it. The death of her dream would be
horribly painful. How, oh how, could she bear it?

Claire turned again and looked at the room. It was more
than four walls, a floor and ceiling filled with furniture. It
was proof of what she could do. Claire had lived here. John
had lived here. Perhaps if her dream came true, one day
they'd stay here together. But that would happen only if
Claire faced her fears, if she was willing to take a risk. She
could do it. She had to.

As Claire reached for the phone, it began to ring.

"Hello." Claire recognized the voice and started to relax.
A moment later, she gripped the chair back to steady herself.

"When? Where?" Claire tried to still the pounding of her heart as she listened to the horrific details. "Try not to worry," she said, though her palms had turned cold with fear. "I'll be there in ten minutes."

It was good that he couldn't see his reflection in the rear-view mirror, John told himself as he pulled onto the Interstate. Chances are, he wouldn't like what he saw: a man who had hurt a wonderful woman and a troubled teenager, a man who failed Life 101. What a fine specimen of humanity he was!

John flicked on the turn signal, passed a car, then moved back into the right lane. The slow lane. How appropriate. His life was definitely in the slow lane. John Moreland, the man who'd made a fortune turning rundown areas into urban paradises, the man that *Time* magazine claimed could mine gold out of what appeared to be pure dross, was a failure. Who would believe it? The reporters from *Time* and all the other magazines saw the John Moreland he chose to project—confident and successful. Even Rick and Angela saw only the outer man. No one knew the real John except . . . John gripped the steering wheel. He didn't want to go there. Literally. But half an hour later, he reached for his cell phone. As painful as it was to admit it, he needed help, and there was one person who might be able to provide it. "Hi, Dad," John said when the call went through. "I know it's short notice, but I wondered if I could visit you tonight."

The momentary silence on the other end of the line told John how unexpected his call was. Would his father hang up or refuse to see him? Since John hadn't made a friendly overture toward him in years, either was a possibility. But instead of rejection, Henry said, "Janet and I are home alone. Come on over." One hurdle down.

The courage John had mustered to make the call began to

falter when he reached the high rise that held his father's penthouse condo. There was still time to turn back. But if he did, John reminded himself, he'd never know whether he could break out of the cycle of unhappiness plaguing the Morelands. John trudged forward, trying to tamp down the feeling of dread. This was his father, for Pete's sake. Even though they hadn't had much of a relationship since the divorce, this was still the man who'd once helped John build towering structures with Lego's. Henry Moreland wasn't an ogre.

John stepped into the elevator. When he knocked on the penthouse door, Janet opened it. "I'm glad to see you." She gave John a smile and brushed her lips across his cheek in a gesture that surprised him. Though it could have been nothing more than a perfunctory greeting, John sensed that Janet was trying to reassure him. Had he been fanciful, he might have said that she was like a medieval lady, bestowing her favor on a knight. But John wasn't facing a battle, simply his father.

"He's in the study." When Janet made no move to accompany him, John realized that perhaps the image of a battle wasn't so farfetched.

Henry Moreland rose from his chair and inclined his head, gesturing John toward the deep leather recliner's mate. "Let's dispense with the pleasantries, shall we?" He settled back into his own chair. "What's wrong?"

John stared at the man who looked so much like him. Henry Moreland's hair was gray, his face etched with lines, but there was no mistaking the resemblance. It was more than physical. John could envision himself treating an unwelcome visitor the same way.

He took a deep breath, trying to relax. Though he had known this wouldn't be an easy conversation, John hadn't expected the hostilities to begin so quickly. When he'd tried to rehearse a speech in the car, every time he'd thought he'd found the best way to begin, he'd stopped. Nothing seemed right. Now all the polite openings he'd considered vanished, and John found himself blurting out the crux of the problem. "I've realized I don't like myself very much."

His father was silent for a moment, as if considering John's words. "I suppose you blame me for that." The look he gave John was long and piercing. It was, John suspected, the same look Henry gave hostile witnesses. No wonder his father was such a successful prosecuting attorney. Had he been on the witness stand and subjected to that stare, John would have told the truth, the whole truth, and nothing but the truth.

"Yeah, I do." That was the truth. "At least partially." And that was the whole truth. He couldn't blame his father for all his mistakes. He might be a chip off the old block, but he was still his own man. The decisions he'd made were his, no matter what had influenced them.

"I suppose I deserve that." John's father looked aside, as if the thought were painful. "I knew your mother was bitter and that she was probably giving you a warped version of our marriage, but I didn't do anything to set the record straight. I left you to believe whatever it was that she was telling you." This time when Henry fixed his gaze on John, his expression was conciliatory. Was this how he treated his own witnesses? "There are always two sides to a story," Henry said.

"Why didn't you talk to me? Why didn't you ask for visitation rights? You're a lawyer. You could have gotten anything you wanted." The words came out more forcefully than John had intended. When his father didn't answer immediately, John said, "I thought it was because you didn't care about me."

Henry shook his head. "That's not true. I did it for your mother. I took so much from Leanne when I divorced her that

I thought it best to leave her with something she cherished, namely you. I didn't want her to have to fight for your love."

John was quiet for a moment, considering his father's words. In all the years since his parents had divorced, he'd never thought that perhaps his father's deliberate distancing had been a gift to his mother. It was true that since Henry had refused to attend important events in John's life—everything from his birthdays to his high school and college graduations—Leanne had become the dominant force in John's life. It hadn't been that way before the divorce. John remembered the special moments he and his father had spent together. The fact that those moments had ended so abruptly had hurt more than he'd admitted.

Henry's decision had been a bad one. It had hurt John, and it certainly hadn't helped Leanne. But now that he understood the reasons why his father had made those choices, John couldn't condemn him. At least not completely.

"You're right about one part," he said. "Mother is still pretty bitter." That was an understatement if there ever was one. Leanne Moreland blamed her ex-husband for everything that went wrong in her life, from the fact that she lived alone to the time that she'd gotten a notice from the IRS announcing she'd failed to pay her estimated tax.

"Leanne won't admit that we were wrong for each other." Henry leaned forward slightly, as if to emphasize his words. "We didn't have anything in common. I was attracted by her beauty, and she liked the idea of being the wife of an up-and-coming lawyer. Not much of a foundation for a lasting relationship." Henry frowned as he spoke the words. "We probably should never have married. I know that now, but, at the same time, I can't regret the years Leanne and I spent together, because that marriage produced you." Henry cleared his throat. It was a distinctly unlawyerly sound. "I'm proud of you, son."

John felt as if he'd waited his whole life for those words, and yet he couldn't accept them. Not tonight. "I'm not very proud of myself right now."

"Do you want to talk about it?"

He shook his head. "It's something I've got to figure out for myself."

Henry reached for the Meerschaum pipe that sat on the table between them, then laid it back, as if suddenly recalling that he'd given up smoking twenty years ago. "You haven't changed," he told his son. "Even as a toddler, you didn't want to ask for help. Somehow you must have decided at a very early age that asking for help was a sign of weakness."

John thought back to the hours he'd spent in the car tonight, wrestling with the idea of calling his father. It was true that he didn't like asking for help. But there was something he had to know before he left here.

"I'll understand if you don't want to answer this, but . . ." He paused, then blurted out the question. "Are you happy?"

"Yes." The smile that lit Henry's face bore witness to the truth of his answer. "It took me a while. I shouldn't have married Kim. She was a rebound romance, the classic mistake. But the years I spent alone after she and I divorced were good for me. They forced me to think about who I was and what I wanted my life to be. And then I met Janet." Henry leaned back in his chair, his expression one of pure contentment. "Janet is the best thing that ever happened to me. She knows all my faults and loves me anyway." For a few seconds, the ticking of the tall clock was the only sound. Then Henry continued. "I've done a lot of things wrong in my life, but marrying Janet was not one of them."

"I'm glad." John rose. He'd gotten his answers. Now he had to make sense of them.

"Will you stay a little longer? I'd like you to get to know Janet."

John shook his head. "Another time. I've got some thinking to do."

An hour later, back in his own condo, John stared at the Manhattan skyline. The buildings were stationary, helping to ground him while his thoughts whirled. His father was happy. John hadn't expected that. For years, he'd listened to his mother disparage Janet and Henry's marriage, claiming they were on the verge of divorce. That had been part of the reason John had shied from the thought of marriage. With a three-time loser as a father, what chance did he have?

The fault was his, John admitted. If he'd spent time with his father and his third wife, he would have seen that they were happy. But he hadn't. He hadn't spent time with them, and he hadn't looked for answers. Instead, he'd accepted his mother's word as truth, even though he knew how skewed her views were. Shame on him.

His father had changed. The question was, could John? His father had learned from his mistakes. Could John? Henry said that Janet loved him, despite his faults. Was John willing to let someone come close enough to see his faults? Would Claire love him anyway? He laughed, a laugh that bore no mirth. There was no need to let anyone come close. John's faults were all too apparent, even from a distance. Claire didn't have to search for them.

And then there was the most difficult question of all: what did he want from life? For the first time, John's future wasn't clear. He'd spent years planning each move, carefully orchestrating his career. But now, when he ought to be basking in his success, everything seemed murky. He wasn't sure what to do next, and that was a distinctly uncomfortable feeling.

John was a man who liked to control his destiny. He needed to control it, and he'd done that remarkably well. But now . . . now things were different. He couldn't control everything, because for the first time, what he wanted was outside his control. For the first time, he didn't want a building or a neighborhood. He wanted a life, and that life involved another person.

Claire. He wanted a life with Claire. What could he offer her?

Chapter Eleven

John winced as he stared out his window. Why did poets wax eloquent over the beauty of the rising sun? The simple fact was, it was painful to look at that blazing ball of light, especially through eyes that were probably bloodshot from lack of sleep. It had been a long time since he had pulled an all-nighter. They'd been rare, even in college. The last one he could remember had been the time he and Rick had worked around the clock to finish their entry for the Peabody Contest. Against formidable odds, they'd won. That had been the jump start that John's career had needed. Last night he'd stayed awake, trying to find a way to jump-start his life. Unfortunately, he hadn't succeeded.

He tugged the drapes closed. As beautiful as he found the Manhattan skyline, John did not appreciate having his retinas singed, and it wasn't as if the sun were providing any inspiration. There had been no aha! moments during the night. The one thing he'd accomplished as he'd paced the floor, stared at the walls, and drank more coffee than a man should consume in a week was that he now knew what he wanted the future to hold. If there were genies in bottles who could make dreams come true, John had his three wishes ready. He'd ask for a life filled with the same kind of happiness that he'd seen on his father's face. He'd ask for a love like the one Dad shared with Janet. He'd ask for Claire.

Unfortunately, there were no genies, at least none that John had ever met. And so, even though he'd finally admitted to himself that he loved Claire, that he wanted to marry her and spend the rest of his life with her, he was faced with a problem that at this particular moment seemed insurmountable. What could he offer her?

John poured another cup of coffee, wrapping his hands around the oversized mug. It was true that he could give her money, fame, and social position. The problem was, although those would be enough to attract most women, they weren't good enough for Claire. External trappings wouldn't bring Claire happiness any more than they'd made his mother's life happy and fulfilled.

John took a deep swallow of coffee as he considered the conundrum of his parents' marriage. By some standards, it should have been successful, not the disaster it had become. Henry Moreland's beautiful wife hadn't brought him any more happiness than his money and social connections had given Leanne Blackburn. When she'd appeared on that stage in Atlantic City, John's mother had told an audience of millions that she wanted to devote her life to helping deaf children. What had happened to that dream? She'd traded it in to become Henry Moreland's wife, and look at her now, alone, bitter, her days filled with nothing more fulfilling than recreational shopping.

John drained the cup. He couldn't let that happen to Claire. He wouldn't ask her to give up her dreams, and—for good or bad—those dreams were centered on the town of Hidden Falls. His dreams were not. His dreams were centered on JBM Enterprises and a job that involved frequent travel and late nights. It was more than a job. It was a lifestyle that gave him a great deal of satisfaction. If he gave it up, what would replace it? Without something of value, John's marriage would be as doomed as his parents'. That kind of sacrifice was as unacceptable as asking Claire to change her life for him. But surely there had to be a way to compromise. The problem was, even quarts of caffeine hadn't cleared his brain enough for him to find that compromise.

The phone rang. John glanced at the caller ID before picking it up. "Hey, Rick, what got you up this early?"

Rick laughed. "You obviously haven't been around kids for a while if you think this is early. Josh has been awake for hours."

John suspected his friend had not called to discuss his son's sleep patterns. "So, what's up? Besides you and Josh, that is."

"I'm not gonna be able to make tennis on Tuesday. Josh's got an appointment with a new doctor in Connecticut, and I figured as long as we were there, we'd visit some of the old carousels."

Carousels. No matter where he turned, someone was talking about them. John was so lost in memories of Claire's plea to restore the Hidden Falls merry-go-round that he almost missed Rick's next words.

"What's that about a hotel in Rhode Island?" He listened for a minute. "You're right. It does sound different. For your sake, I hope that different doesn't translate into awful."

As he hung up the phone, John's thoughts returned to Claire. She would be a great general manager for Fairlawn. Though he'd been skeptical initially, John no longer harbored any doubts about that. But Claire wanted—and deserved—more. She wanted marriage, children, and a home-for-dinner-every-day father for those children. How was he going to manage that and still run JBM Enterprises?

Perhaps more caffeine would help. John was reaching for the coffee pot when the phone rang again.

"John, it's Claire."

Though he started to smile, the distress he heard in her voice made his lips flatten. "What's wrong?"

Her words came quickly, as if she'd repeated them a dozen times. "Ryan was in a car accident. He and his friends stole some beer, then went for a drive." Claire took a shallow breath. "The car flipped over."

Oh, no! As images of a tangled wreck flashed before him, John managed to ask, "Is Ryan okay?" *Please, please,* he prayed silently, *let the boy be all right.*

"He was lucky. They all were." When John realized that he had a death grip on the phone, he forced himself to relax as Claire continued. "Ryan has broken ribs and a mild concussion. The others were released, but the doctors want to keep him in the hospital another day for observation."

"I'll be there as soon as I can."

Hospitals were not John's favorite spot. Of course, he doubted anyone relished a visit to them, despite the fact that the walls were no longer antiseptic green or the floors drab linoleum. Though he'd thought he might meet Claire or another of the teachers here, the nurse who'd pointed the way to the boy's room told John that he had no visitors.

"Hello, Ryan." John tried to keep his voice light as he walked inside. That wasn't easy when the teenager's bandaged head and the IV in his arm made his condition appear more serious than Claire had indicated.

Ryan, who seemed to be strapped down flat on his back, turned his head slightly. "Go away," he snarled. "I don't want to see you. You're not my friend."

John couldn't complain about the welcome. It was no more than he deserved. He'd spent the entire drive wondering whether he was to blame for Ryan's accident. Had the boy's anger with John been the reason he'd turned to beer? Had the temptation of temporary oblivion been so strong that he'd drunk enough to ignore everything he'd been taught about riding with an impaired driver? The timing couldn't have been coincidental, especially not when coupled with Ryan's obvious hostility. "That's a shame," John said evenly, "because I consider you my friend."

Ryan's eyes narrowed. "You weren't my friend yesterday."

Though it was evident that he was an unwelcome guest, John pulled a chair next to the bed. "You're wrong there, Ryan. Friends help each other, but that doesn't mean that they always like what the other one says."

The silence stretched as Ryan appeared to be considering John's words. "I'm not a failure."

He spoke so softly that John had to strain to hear him. As the teenager's declaration registered, John felt a moment of intense regret. Was that what Ryan thought he'd meant yesterday? Even though he knew he hadn't uttered the word, had there been something in John's voice or even his demeanor that had made Ryan believe he considered him a failure? Why, oh why had John let the boy run away? Perhaps if he'd chased Ryan and forced him to listen, the drinking and driving and its dreadful aftermath would never have occurred. John took a deep breath. There was no way he could undo yesterday. All he could do was try to ensure that it would never recur.

"Of course you aren't a failure," he told Ryan. "I'm the one who failed if what I said made you feel that way."

"You've never failed. You've had a perfect life." There was no doubt about it. Ryan was angry. If anything, the anger seemed more intense than yesterday, perhaps because it had festered while he had been lying in this hospital bed.

John kept his voice low and even. "If you think that my life is perfect, I deserve an Oscar. The truth is, I envy you."

"Sure thing. And pigs fly."

"You can scoff all you want, but you had something I didn't. You had a father who was there when you were growing up. From everything you've told me, I think it's safe to say that you had a father who wasn't afraid to show you that he cared about you. I didn't."

"Yeah, but your dad didn't die." Ryan's scowl deepened.

"No, he didn't. But he did walk out of my life when I was fourteen, and he wasn't around very much before then."

Rather than respond, Ryan switched on the TV. John grabbed the remote and clicked it off, then moved it out of Ryan's reach. As he'd hoped, the minor power struggle loosened Ryan's vocal chords. "Do you expect me to feel sorry for you?"

"Nope. I don't expect anything. I'm simply telling you that, even though you may not believe it, you're lucky. You're lucky that you had good parents, and you're lucky that yesterday's stupidity didn't cost you your life." The image of a freshly dug grave and mourners standing next to it had haunted John on the drive to the hospital. Thank goodness the boys had been wearing seatbelts and hadn't been thrown out of the vehicle.

Ryan did not appear thankful. Instead, he honed in on one word. "I'm not stupid," he said, and this time his voice was almost a shout.

"What you did was. Drinking and driving is stupid."

Ryan struggled to sit up, his frustration with the restraints obvious. It was also clear that if he could, he'd hit John. "You don't understand. I just wanted to have a little fun."

"There are other ways to have fun." Less dangerous ones.

"In Hidden Falls?" Ryan didn't bother to hide his sarcasm. "Yeah, right."

The words echoed through John's brain as he drove the few blocks to Claire's house. What did teenagers do for fun here? The undersized mall didn't appear to be much of a gathering place, and the films at the one movie theater were at least a year old. Hidden Falls seemed as devoid of activities as it was of businesses. Maybe it was good that the high school was being closed. Maybe the new regional school would be located in a more prosperous area. Maybe they'd even build after-hours and weekend activities into the plans for the school. Or maybe . . . A rush of adrenaline flowed through John as an idea began to take shape. Surely it wasn't only sleep deprivation that was making this seem like the solution to so many problems.

"Thanks for calling me," John said as Claire opened the door and ushered him into the house where he'd once lived. Though his fingers were itching to start making notes, he couldn't leave Hidden Falls without seeing Claire. "I feel as if I'm at least partially responsible."

As Claire studied him for a moment, John let his eyes feast on her. Her hair looked as if she'd forgotten to brush it, and the circles under her eyes told John she'd gotten little sleep. Despite that, Claire was still the most beautiful woman he'd ever seen. "Did you meet Ryan's mother at the hospital?" she asked.

"No, why?"

"It's probably just as well you didn't see her. At least last night, Alice was blaming you for the accident."

John nodded, relieved that the conversation remained focused on Ryan. There were so many things he wanted to tell Claire, so many questions he wanted to ask her, but this was not the right time. "I could have handled the situation with Ryan better, just as I could have handled our discussion of the carousel better." He needed to explain why he'd reacted as he had, but he couldn't do that now, not when he didn't have all the answers. So much was at stake that he couldn't risk blurting out half-formed ideas and having her reject them. If he had only one chance—and John suspected that was the case—he had to do everything he could to ensure success.

Claire swallowed deeply, and if he hadn't known better, John would have said that she was nervous. But the Claire he knew was never nervous. She swallowed again, and this time John noticed that she was pleating her shirt tail between her fingers. For some reason, Claire was ill at ease.

"We need to talk," she said. "There's something I have . . ." If John had had any doubts about the seriousness of the situation, the expression in Claire's eyes would have dispelled them. He didn't know whether she wanted to talk about Ryan or the carousel or the way he and she had parted. All John knew was that he wasn't ready.

"John! I thought I heard your voice." Glinda's lavender scent filled the room as she rushed in, raising her arms to hug him. "I didn't know you'd come back."

Thank you, Glinda. This time John's relief was palpable. Whatever it was Claire wanted to discuss, it would now have to wait. Glinda's arrival had spared John, and for that he would be eternally grateful. "I just came to see Ryan," he explained. "I need to get back to New Jersey."

How many times had he said that? This time it wasn't a convenient excuse to escape. This time there were things that could only be done there. And maybe, if everything went the way he hoped, this would be the last time he'd pronounce those words.

Glinda gave John a look that penetrated more deeply than an X-ray. "What about Fairlawn? I heard some nonsensical rumors that you had a change of heart."

Had her X-ray eyes seen inside him? Surely not. When she spoke of a change of heart, Glinda was referring to the possibility of abandoning the project, not his feelings about Claire and his plans for the future.

"The hotel's on hold right now, pending a couple things," John said as smoothly as he could. Those "things" were nothing more than half-formed ideas. They might be crazy. They might be impractical. Then, again, they might be just what he and Claire and Hidden Falls needed.

John wasn't superstitious, but he knew better than to discuss anything of this magnitude until he had all the facts. He turned to Claire. "We'll talk about it when I return."

"And when will that be?" Normally sweet-tempered Glinda fired the question at him.

"Why, for your birthday, of course."

When he pulled the car into the garage, John realized that the drive home was a blur. He must have paid tolls. He must have made the correct turns, but he couldn't remember any of the details. All he remembered were the images that kept whirling through his brain, images of Ryan lying in the hospital bed, of John's mother's brittle smile, and—most painful of all—of the emotion he'd seen reflected in Claire's eyes. It would take Superman to solve those problems, and John Moreland was no Superman. Still, he had to try. The fatigue that he'd kept at bay all day was taking effect, and he knew he'd crash soon. But first he had three calls to make.

The first was easy. She picked up on the second ring, giving him her normal cheerful greeting.

"Angela, I'm glad I caught you." John had no time for pleasantries. "I have a new project for you. Here's what I want." He started to explain, then said, "You'd better sit down. You may never hear this from me again." As she chuckled and announced that she was indeed seated, John said, "I want it, no matter what it costs." Angela's gasp was worth every extra penny he'd have to spend.

He hesitated before he picked up the phone again. This call would be more difficult, and yet it was essential. John closed his eyes, picturing all that was at stake. If he could do everything himself, he would, but—as much as he hated to admit it—some things were beyond his control. He looked at the phone, reminding himself that it was an inanimate object, not a cobra poised to strike. He could do it. He could overcome a lifetime of habits. He could form the words. John took a deep breath and punched in the number.

"Dad," he said when the familiar voice answered, "I'm afraid I may already be too late, but I need your help again."

John held his breath, waiting for the response. There was no recrimination, not even a gentle "I told you so." Instead, Henry Moreland listened carefully, asked a few pointed questions, then promised his assistance.

"I think Janet and I may visit a few friends," he said, his voice warm with enthusiasm. "It's more difficult to refuse a request in person, especially when you bring your wife along. You might want to remember that."

John would, if he ever had a wife. It was true that he was doing his best to have something to offer Claire, but, unpalatable as the thought was, failure was always a possibility.

As he hung up the phone, John glanced longingly at the bedroom. He needed sleep. Desperately. The last call could wait. Nothing would change if he didn't make it until tomorrow morning. He shook his head. The arguments were valid, but he knew he was hesitating, because this was the riskiest call. Though it wasn't directly connected to Claire as the others had been, John was certain that if he could resolve this problem, his marriage would be a better one. With a sigh, he booted his computer, then entered a search argument. Half an hour later, he picked up the phone again.

"I have a meeting tomorrow afternoon," he said. "It's a fairly long drive, but it should be pretty. Anyway, I wondered if I could convince you to go with me." He who never babbled was babbling. "I'll buy you dinner afterwards."

The moment of silence lengthened to the point where he was certain she'd refuse.

"Okay," she said at last.

John smiled. "Thanks, Mother."

"I know it's a cliché," Ruby said, "but you look like you've lost your best friend." She sat at Claire's side in the faculty dining room, drinking black coffee and looking longingly at the jelly donuts.

"That's impossible. You're my best friend." Admittedly, at this point Ruby was a much too perceptive best friend. She wasn't supposed to realize how upset Claire was by what had happened—and what hadn't happened—with John.

Ruby reached for a donut, then pulled her hand back as if the pastry were red-hot. "Six months ago I was your best friend, but now I think the title belongs to John."

Claire looked around. Where were the other teachers when you needed them? Everyone appeared engrossed in private conversations. Since rescue did not appear imminent, she decided to bluff. "John Moreland?"

Ruby snickered. "Is there another John in your life?"

Why not admit it? Ruby could be almost as persistent as Glinda. "There are no Johns in my life."

"Exactly what I suspected." Ruby reached out, and this time her hand snagged a donut. "What happened?" she asked after she'd swallowed the first bite. "Don't tell me that he's just a business associate. I've seen the way you two look at each other."

Claire tried to hide behind her coffee mug. When she'd taken a long swallow and busied herself by placing the mug carefully on the table, as if the fate of the world depended on the mug's handle being at precisely ninety degrees to the edge of the table, she looked up at Ruby. "That may have been true once," Claire admitted, "but it's over now. John's gone from Hidden Falls and my life." All the soul searching she'd done, all the courage she'd mustered had been for naught. John hadn't given her an opportunity to tell him she loved him. He hadn't given her a chance to tell him anything.

Ruby lowered her voice. "What happened?"

"I'm not sure, and that's the worst part. All those seminars on problem solving tell you that you can't fix a problem if you can't identify it. They were right."

John had been exhausted and obviously preoccupied after his visit to the hospital. It was true that he'd apologized for the way he'd refused to finance the carousel, but, Claire reminded herself, he hadn't said he'd changed his mind. He regretted the delivery, not the message. Claire could accept that. What she couldn't accept was the way John kept disappearing. Whenever there was a problem, he ran from it. She'd seen the expression in his eyes when she'd told him they needed to talk. His reaction had said more clearly than words that he didn't want to entertain any kind of discussion with her. Claire had no defenses against such a blatant dismissal.

Ruby pushed the donut away. "You two are perfect for each other."

"Unfortunately, John doesn't feel that way."

It was not the best week of her life, Claire reflected as she made her way to her last class. In fact, it was a definite contender for the worst. Ryan had been released from the hospital but was so surly at school that he'd been sent to the principal's office. His mother acted as if the problem were somehow Claire's fault. And now, this. Gerry Feltz wanted to see her after school.

"Thanks for coming," the principal said when Claire had taken the seat across from him. Though he smiled genially, there was something about his expression that told Claire this was not a casual conversation.

"I've been working with the other principals," he said, "figuring out what our staff needs will be once the schools are consolidated." That was sooner than Claire had expected. After all, the location of the new complex hadn't yet been finalized. That decision would undoubtedly impact some teachers' willingness to transfer.

Gerry leaned forward, smiling. "It's amazing the way things are working out." He smiled again. "I have to admit that I was worried for a while, but now I'm really glad that you took that position with John Moreland. The other principals and I have agreed that, even though each of the schools currently has an FCS teacher, the new one will need only two."

Even though it would mean larger classes, Claire couldn't fault the logic. Reduced staff size would help ensure that the promised tax cuts were achieved.

Gerry continued, "Joanna Simpson is a shoe-in for the first one. That leaves you and Marge Pearson. Marge has more seniority and an extra certification." Claire knew that. She also knew that Marge had been talking about early retirement for the past five years.

Gerry's smile became almost a grin. "When Marge heard about your new job, she agreed to stay on for at least another year. Isn't it great when things work out?"

"Yeah. Great."

Claire tried not to frown as she walked home. *How much greater could it get?* Her intuition told her that John was going to abandon Fairlawn. That meant she had no job, and the town had no future. Great. Really great. This week had definitely won the award for Worst Ever.

She increased her pace, wishing she had worn her jogging shoes. If she were running, she could generate more endorphins. Maybe then the future would look brighter. As she turned the corner onto Maple, Claire straightened her shoulders. Glinda claimed that she could control her future. If ever there was a time to start, it was now. There was no point in wallowing in self-pity. That would accomplish nothing.

Claire took a deep breath. She wasn't the only one affected by the school's closing. All of Hidden Falls was already feeling the effects. Claire had seen the way people had lost their enthusiasm and the way minor disagreements made tempers flare. Everyone dreaded the changes that the next year would bring.

She took another deep cleansing breath. She might not be able to do anything about her job, at least not today, but there had to be something she could do for the town. Hidden Falls needed a revival. It didn't have to be a big one, but it had to be something everyone could believe in. The people needed something to unite them.

Claire began to smile as an idea took root. Of course! Hidden Falls' residents could restore the carousel. Even John had admitted that was a good idea. When she'd first thought about it, Claire had envisioned a single financier. But it didn't have to be one person with deep pockets who paid for the restoration. The whole town could be involved. Claire laughed in sheer delight as she realized that the whole town *should* be involved. Was that why John had refused to pay for the restoration? Had he realized what Claire had missed, that if the townspeople were part of the project, they'd have a sense of ownership? This could be exactly what Hidden Falls needed. Working on the merry-go-round could restore more than the old painted ponies. It could restore the town's civic pride.

"Glinda!" Claire called to her grandmother as she opened the door. "Get your phone book. I've got a project for you."

"Where on earth are you taking me?" Leanne asked as they made yet another turn. They'd traveled west on Interstate 78 for close to an hour, exiting in the midst of the famous New Jersey horse country. Though his mother had asked where they were going, John had refused to answer, merely suggesting that she enjoy the scenery. At this time of the year, with the grass once again green and the fruit trees blooming, the countryside exuded pastoral beauty. On another day, John would have found it restful. Today, his nerves were wound tighter than the proverbial cheap watch.

"I thought you said you had a meeting." Leanne's voice was becoming querulous.

"I do. Just because there are horse farms out here doesn't mean it's the end of civilization." If everything went the way he hoped, it wouldn't be the end of anything. It would be a beginning. But he couldn't tell his mother that. If she knew what he intended, she'd manufacture a dozen excuses why it wouldn't work. Thank goodness, they were close to their destination. John wasn't certain how much longer he could dodge Leanne's questions. Five minutes later, he turned into the long drive that was marked by a simple white sign bearing one word: HARLOW'S. If his mother recognized the name, she gave no indication.

The drive curved twice before it reached the large redbrick Georgian building with six imposing columns. What a first impression! The building was even more beautiful than the pictures on the Web site. Harlow's claimed to be the preeminent school of its type, and if the campus was any indication, they had not exaggerated.

"What do they do here?" John's mother asked when he parked the car. Excellent! She had no idea. John was counting on the element of surprise to overcome her resistance.

"You'll see." He opened the door and ushered Leanne out of the car. As he'd arranged with the administrator, no one greeted them. That would come later, if his mother agreed. Their destination, John had been told, was behind the building. He led his mother along the carefully groomed path, then watched her reaction as they rounded the corner.

Hidden by the house was a playground filled with the latest in children's equipment. Two dozen boys and girls crowded the swings, slides, and jungle gym, their enthusiasm evident. It was a scene that was undoubtedly being repeated at hundreds of school playgrounds across the state. The only difference was the silence. Instead of the shouts and shrieks that filled most playgrounds, there were soft grunts and squeaks and hands moving at an almost furious pace.

Leanne's eyes widened as she watched one of the boys sign to his companion. "Oh, John!" Tears filled her eyes, and he knew she realized why the children were not speaking. They were all deaf.

"C'mon, Mother. There are some kids here who need you."

Chapter Twelve

"Can you believe that tomorrow's the big day?" Ruby stirred a packet of sweetener into her iced tea, then looked up at Claire. The two women had spent their after-school time running errands. Now, their cars loaded with last-minute purchases and their feet tired from standing in line, they were indulging in one of their favorite pastimes: letting the staff at the diner wait on them.

"Glinda's more excited than I've ever seen her." Claire sipped her milkshake. Unlike Ruby, she wasn't dieting to fit into a bridal gown. "I just hope the weather holds." When Claire had started planning her grandmother's birthday celebration, she had envisioned a formal dinner catered by herself with the assistance of the Gourmet Wannabes. But as the guest list grew and grew, she'd accepted the impracticality of trying to seat two hundred people and had suggested a cookout for the whole town. That had created its own set of logistical challenges. Though spacious, her grandmother's backyard would not accommodate so many people. It had been Ruby who'd recommended using the school grounds, pointing out that there'd be no problem with parking and that all they'd have to do was rent some tables, chairs, and a tent. Or two. Or six.

Ruby's eyes sparkled with mischief. "I know Glinda doesn't want gifts, but I'm tempted to give her a scepter. You know, like her namesake in *The Wizard of Oz.*" Ruby had already suggested that Glinda wear a tiara.

Claire smiled, thinking of her grandmother carrying a wand with a sparkly star on top. If anyone in Hidden Falls could pull that off without looking silly, it was Glinda. "I think you've got the namesake bit backwards, but I get the idea. If you do find a magic wand, buy two. I could use one myself." One with a lot of magic. It would take more than an average supply to fix everything that was wrong in Claire's life.

Fortunately, Ruby seemed to think Claire was referring to the carousel restoration. "Don't sell yourself short," Ruby said. "What you've accomplished is close to miraculous. I still can't believe the way the town has banded together."

Claire took another sip of her milkshake. The carousel project had been a lifesaver for her, giving her something to focus on other than the school and John. Thanks to it, thoughts of John intruded only a thousand or so times a day.

"C'mon, Ruby. You shouldn't be surprised. If there's anything we teachers know, it's how to motivate kids. Adults are just big kids." She wouldn't say she'd used child psychology. After all, it was basic human psychology to vie for the alpha role within a group. All Claire had done was stimulate the desire.

"I love the idea of getting different organizations to sponsor the horses. That's added a little bit of rivalry."

"A little bit?" Claire chuckled. "Look at the way the teachers reacted. They're determined that we'll have the best animal on the merry-go-round."

To Claire's surprise, when she'd done more research on

the Hidden Falls carousel, she'd discovered that it was what carousel fans called a menagerie, meaning that it had other animals in addition to horses. The town's merry-go-round boasted a pair each of elephants, bears, giraffes, and ostriches, plus eight pairs of horses. When the teachers had heard that, they'd insisted on adopting one of the elephants. Elephants, someone had pointed out, had incredible memories, and that's what they hoped their students would have, too. Not to be outdone, the students had started organizing car washes so they could sponsor the other elephant.

"You don't need a magic wand," Ruby said. "You've done an incredible job."

"With a lot of help from my friends." Even Claire had been impressed with all that had been accomplished in the last two weeks. As she had hoped, the people of Hidden Falls had rallied, once they'd heard about the plans for the carousel. As of yesterday morning, all but three of the animals had been found. The majority had been languishing in garages and barns, collecting dust. Perhaps that was the reason the owners had agreed to loan them to the town. It was amazing what the promise of free restoration and a bronze plaque listing their names would do to encourage people to clean out their garages.

Locating the horses had been the first challenge. The second was finding a way to pay for restoring them. When she'd realized that JBM Enterprises would not fund the restoration, Claire had devised the idea of asking various organizations to sponsor an animal in return for being allowed to name it. That part of the project had been more successful than Claire had dared to hope. The friendly rivalry that ensued was contributing to the overall excitement as well as the town's sense of ownership. Everywhere Claire went, people were talking about the carousel. Frowns caused by the school's closing had changed to smiles.

That left only one hurdle, and it was a major one. Somehow, Claire had to find the money to construct a building to house the merry-go-round and to purchase the mechanical parts that turned the platform and made the horses move up and down. Those, as she had guessed, were not inexpensive, nor was the sound system she needed if she was going to recreate the original carousel experience. It had been Steve who'd suggested applying for a grant.

"That fiancé of yours is a gem," she told Ruby.

Ruby smiled as she fingered her engagement ring. "I know." When she looked up, her expression was serious. "Oh, Claire, I wish . . ."

Claire didn't have to be a mind reader to know what Ruby was going to say. Both she and Glinda had made no secret of the fact that they thought Claire and John belonged together. If they had their way, Hidden Falls would celebrate two weddings this summer.

"Please don't start on that again. It's obviously not meant to be." Claire gave her milkshake glass a little push. The chocolate malt had lost its appeal. A few minutes later, she picked up the check and walked the few feet to the cash register. Her life, which had once seemed so settled, was in turmoil, and she had no magic wand to fix it. Although it was true that she was enjoying the work she was doing for the carousel restoration, that was volunteer work. It wouldn't help Claire pay for groceries or make car payments. *Another year*, she reminded herself. She had another year before her teaching contract ended. A lot could happen in a year.

What was that old saying about one day at a time? Claire straightened her shoulders as she walked to the car. It was good advice. She'd take each day as it came. The problem was, those days seemed long and lonely without John. It had been only two weeks since she'd seen him, but at times she'd feared they would never end. At other times she feared the end, for if she was right, this would be John's final trip to Hidden Falls. Once Glinda's party was over, Claire would have nothing to look forward to.

Even the excitement of the carousel project hadn't been able to dissipate the malaise she felt every time she thought of John and realized how bleak their future was. *Be honest, Claire. There will be no future unless you take Glinda's advice and create it.* He'd be here tomorrow. Somehow, though every minute of the day seemed to be programmed with activities, she would find time to talk to him. It was her only chance.

John pushed the CD into the changer, waiting for the music to fill the car. He couldn't say why he'd bought a country CD, other than the fact that the unfamiliar songs might help keep him awake. It had nothing to do with this being Claire's favorite type of music. Nothing at all. The simple fact was, one of these days he needed to get some sleep, and in the meantime, he needed something to discourage drowsiness. Oh, he hadn't pulled any more all-nighters, but trying to get months of work done in two weeks had required extra effort. A lot of extra effort.

Fortunately, he hadn't had to do it alone. He'd spent hours on the phone, calling in favors. As Chris LeDoux sang about a cowboy's hat, John started to smile. This project was like that hat, composed of a number of gifts, each from a special person, and that made the result both unique and priceless. Always in the past, John had been the leader, the one calling all the shots. This time his friends had worked with him, providing suggestions that had been invaluable.

Rick and Angela had an amazing network of contacts, and they hadn't hesitated to pull strings for him. His father had done what he'd promised, visiting colleagues, persuading and—when needed—twisting arms. The real surprise had been Janet. John hadn't known that she'd worked on Wall Street before she married Henry Moreland. He felt more than a twinge of shame that he hadn't bothered to learn anything about his new stepmother, especially considering how long she and Dad had been married. That would change, once this weekend was over. In the meantime, Janet had proven invaluable in helping him organize the consortium he needed.

The only person close to him who hadn't been involved was his mother, and John wasn't complaining about that, since Leanne was spending her days at Harlow's. It was too soon to know whether she'd become a permanent volunteer or even a member of the staff, but the lilt in her voice when she called John each night to talk about "her" children gave him hope.

The pieces were fitting together. All except for one. John glanced at his watch, then checked his cell phone for the hundredth time, making sure that it was turned on. If everything went as he hoped, he'd have that last piece today. Then all that remained would be Claire. What would she say when she learned what he'd done? What would she say when he presented his plan for their future? John tightened his grip on the steering wheel. What would Claire say when he asked her the most important question of all?

He took a deep breath, exhaling slowly. He'd have his answers by sundown.

"You certainly have a beautiful day for the party." Though the celebration didn't begin until noon, Claire and Ruby had been at the school grounds since early morning, supervising the placement of tents, tables, and the decorations that would make this a day to remember. Dozens of coolers were filled with food and beverages, and the workers were setting up the large grill where Steve and several of his cohorts would cook hotdogs and hamburgers. All that remained was the sound system. And the guests.

At Claire's insistence, her grandmother had stayed at home. But now, obviously unable to contain her curiosity, Glinda had arrived. She walked from tent to tent, admiring the silk flowers Ruby had draped around the poles, smiling when she saw the tablecloths in every color of the rainbow. The best parties, Claire had announced when she and Glinda had first started planning her birthday celebration, had a theme. It hadn't been difficult to find one for this. In honor of Glinda's *Wizard of Oz* name, her party was called "Over the Rainbow."

Glinda clasped her hands together. "It probably sounds silly, but when I look at all this, I feel as if I were sixteen again."

"You don't look a day older."

Both Claire and Glinda spun around at the sound of John's voice. When had he arrived? Claire hadn't expected him for at least another hour. Truthfully, she hadn't been convinced that he would come. She'd half expected him to call with an excuse, but there he stood, a foot away from her, looking more handsome than ever. It wasn't fair. The man had circles under his eyes, yet they only made him seem more distinguished. Claire knew that her own sleepless nights had had a far less attractive effect.

"Flattery will get you everything, young man." Glinda's voice was almost coquettish as she smiled at John.

"What about flowers?" He drew a box from behind his back and presented it to her with a flourish.

As Glinda opened the box and withdrew a rainbow-hued corsage, she raised an eyebrow. "This is beautiful, John. But what about Claire? Don't you have any flowers for her?"

He shook his head. "It's not her birthday. But don't worry, Glinda. I'll see if I can find something to salvage her day."

What on earth did the man have in mind? And why did he think the day would need salvaging? This was Glinda's day, and it was going to be perfect, unless one all-too-attractive man continued to stand there ignoring her. Glinda might be the guest of honor, but John could have acknowledged Claire's presence. As far as she could tell, he hadn't even looked at her. Why had she wasted all that time choosing a dress and carefully arranging her hair in a French braid?

"In case you haven't noticed," Claire said with more than a little asperity, "I'm right here, and I'm not deaf." Her parents had done that once, talking about her as if she weren't present. It had annoyed her then, and it annoyed her even more now. John was being rude. Inexcusably so.

"I'm sorry, Claire." He wore a slightly sheepish expression that might have melted Claire's heart had it not been followed by a surreptitious look at his watch. "It's simply that I was overcome by your grandmother's beauty." He delivered the line in such melodramatic tones that Claire couldn't help smiling.

Glinda wagged a finger at him. "Didn't your mother teach you to tell the truth?"

"Yes, ma'am, she did." More melodrama. Was the man trying out for a fifth-rate play?

"If she did that, she probably also taught you the importance of being polite to your hostess. That's Claire, in case you weren't certain."

"I assure you that I have every intention of being polite to your granddaughter, right after she gives me some of her raspberry tea." John glanced at his cell phone, as if assuring himself that it was turned on. Claire started to fume. *First the watch; now the cell phone. How obvious could he make it that he didn't want to be here?*

Apparently unconcerned, Glinda gave John a warm smile. "I'll leave you two alone while I greet some of my guests." Cars had begun to line the street as people made their way toward the tents, directed by Ruby.

When they reached the kitchen tent, Claire poured a glass of tea for John and tried to let her annoyance subside. The melodramatic speeches, the odd smiles he'd given her when he talked about salvaging her day and being polite to her, the apparent preoccupation with his cell phone weren't normal behavior for John. The problem was, Claire had no idea what had caused the changes. Perhaps it was only sleep deprivation. As much as she wanted to believe that, she didn't. It was more likely John had started a new project and was engrossed in it.

"Is there anything I can do to help?" he asked when he'd emptied the glass. Though his question was directed to Claire, he was staring outside the tent, as if looking for something or someone.

"Would you mind carrying the punch bowl to that tent?" Claire bit back a caustic comment as she gestured toward the tent that would house the buffet line. "It's a bit heavy."

"No problem." John stifled a yawn before he picked up the cut glass bowl. A minute later he was back. "Is there anything else?" He touched his cell phone.

"Yes, there is." Claire moved a step closer to him and fixed her gaze on him. "You can answer a question for me. Why did you bother to come today when it's clear that you don't want to be here?" She had had such high hopes for the day, but they'd been shattered by John's obvious distraction.

His eyes widened, and he shook his head slightly, as if trying to clear it. "What do you mean, I don't want to be here?" The man looked genuinely surprised by her question.

"The constant checking of your watch, looking at your cell phone, and yawning are pretty good indications that you're bored here." Although, Claire had to admit, the yawning might have something to do with being tired. Still, there was no excuse for the others.

John shook his head again. "You've taken two plus two and gotten five."

"And what should I have gotten?" When her question was met with silence, Claire's anger increased. "What am I supposed to think? I know how you feel about this 'little town in the middle of nowhere.' I know how hopeless you think we are." Claire took a step closer and placed an accusatory finger on his chest. "I agree that you're entitled to your opinions, even though they're wrong. But you are not entitled to spoil Glinda's birthday just because you don't like being here." Though the morning breeze was chilly, it did nothing to cool Claire's temper.

John's eyes flashed with something that might have been anger. "You're wrong, Claire. You don't know how I feel." She saw him start to look at his watch, then—with an obvious effort—stop. "You're right about one thing, though. It's my fault that you don't know how I feel. I haven't told you." This time when John looked around the school grounds, Claire had the sense that he was searching for something different than before. "This isn't the time or place I would have chosen," he said, his voice tinged with regret, "but I can't wait any longer. Where can we go where we won't be overheard?"

Claire's heart skipped a beat as every dream she'd woven around this man flashed before her. *Could it be that he felt as she did? Did he want seclusion to tell her he loved her?* An instant later, reality came crashing back. She was doing it again: adding two and two and getting five.

You can create your future. Glinda's words echoed in Claire's brain. She had worried about finding the right time. Perhaps this was it. Claire had promised herself that she wouldn't let John leave Hidden Falls without knowing that she loved him. Though, as he said, this wasn't the time or place she would have chosen, this could be her only opportunity. The time was now. *What about the place?* Claire thought for a second. The school grounds were far from the ideal location for a declaration of love. Wasn't that supposed to occur with moonlight and roses? Neither one was available now. Still, she and John couldn't leave the party, not with the trickle of guests turning into a steady stream. She turned toward him. "The steps on the other side of the main building are out of the way."

They walked in silence, and Claire wondered whether John felt as uneasy as she did. Now that the moment had arrived, she wasn't certain she had enough courage to follow through with her intentions. Somehow, someway she'd do it, but first, she would let John explain his apparent distraction.

When they reached the concrete steps, she sat down. There was no reason to have this conversation standing up, especially when her legs felt like over-steamed asparagus. Claire patted the concrete, inviting John to sit next to her. Though she didn't expect him to settle so close that she could smell the faint scent of raspberry tea on his breath, he did, and Claire's traitorous memory replayed the magic of being held in his arms and tasting his kisses. *Not now! Maybe never again.*

John stared into the distance, then turned back to look at Claire. "You were right to think I didn't appreciate Hidden Falls when I first saw it," he told her. "I didn't. I didn't want to be here, and I most definitely did not plan to make this my home."

Why was John using the past tense? He'd made it clear from the beginning that he'd be here for the length of the project and not one minute more. Had he changed his mind? Claire felt her eyes widen in surprise. *Was this what John wanted to tell her?*

"I've always been a city guy. I couldn't live without my daily fix of automobile exhaust, or so I thought."

He was still using the past tense. The tiny bubble of hope that had lodged deep inside Claire began to grow. It would be wonderful if John lived here. They could continue to work together and maybe, just maybe . . .

"It took a while," he said, "but I began to appreciate the

town. Being here made me realize that there's more to life than a fast pace." His gaze was steady, his expression inscrutable as he said, "I don't know when it happened, but I do know why." He opened his mouth, as if to continue the explanation, then closed it.

Though Claire longed to know why he had changed his mind, the firm line of John's lips told her she would not get an answer. Instead, she asked, "Does this mean you're going to proceed with the renovations of Fairlawn?" When he'd told Glinda that the project was on hold, Claire had believed the hold was permanent. This was one time when she wouldn't mind being wrong.

"I'd like to continue, but that depends on a couple things." As Claire raised an eyebrow, encouraging him to elaborate, John said, "I have some new ideas for Fairlawn. We'll talk about them later." He looked at his watch.

"There you go again."

"Sorry. I thought I might get a call this morning."

A call from whom? About what? Claire knew better than to ask. Instead she looked at her own watch. "Morning's almost over. It's five minutes to noon." In five minutes Glinda's party would officially begin.

"Yeah." There was no ignoring the disappointment in John's voice and the accompanying slump of his shoulders. He took a deep breath, then looked at Claire again. "You were right. Hidden Falls is worth saving." He paused for a second. "That's the reason I bought the old mill."

Claire blinked in surprise. Though she would never have guessed this was what John wanted to tell her, it was wonderful news. He wouldn't tear down the old building. Claire knew that instinctively. "I thought it had been sold to a condo developer."

"Let's just say that he was persuaded it would not be a good investment."

"And you think it is?" It had been only a few weeks since John had declared Hidden Falls hopeless.

"It could be."

Claire was tempted to pinch herself so that she'd know she wasn't dreaming. "It's a great idea, John, but I don't understand. What changed your mind?"

His lips curved in an ironic smile. "Are only women allowed to change their minds?" When Claire shook her head, he continued. "Some people might say I'm having a midlife crisis, but I don't think I'm old enough to qualify for that. The truth is, I've decided to take the company in a different direction. You could call it follow-through. Instead of doing the renovations and then leaving a project, we'll be involved in running some of them."

"But how will you manage?" Claire knew John already spent seventy percent of this time traveling.

"I realized that I can't be as hands-on as I've been in the past. I need to delegate more. My dad told me that."

Claire hoped her surprise wasn't obvious. Something had definitely happened to John in the last two weeks if the man who'd been estranged from his father was now taking his advice.

"My plan is to hire a general manager for each project and turn the day-to-day operations over to them. It's sort of like the way you were going to run Fairlawn."

Were. The past tense had returned, but in a most unwelcome context. It sounded as if John no longer envisioned Claire at Fairlawn.

"If all goes the way I hope," he continued, "I'll live here. It's certainly not rocket science, but I realized that the helicopter I was planning to use to bring guests in could also be used to take me to job sites."

He had everything figured out. Claire knew she ought to be thrilled. Part of her was thrilled, the part that knew this would be good for Hidden Falls. But the other part couldn't help notice that she was conspicuously absent from John's plans.

Swallowing deeply, she asked, "What are you going to do with the mill?"

"Turn it into shops and restaurants and something for the kids to do after school. I don't know what that's going to be, but I imagine Ryan Francis can give me some ideas."

So could Claire, though John didn't appear to recognize that. He rose and stood before her, a wry smile on his face. "I have to admit that I get a kick out of the idea of renovating a family heirloom, so to speak. I also have first right of refusal on the old boarding houses."

Those buildings occupied the block directly across from the mill. This was no whim. John had thought of everything. "Room for expansion."

"Exactly. So, what do you think of the idea?" There was a hint of uncertainty in John's voice that surprised Claire. How could he think she'd be anything but thrilled by his plan? Hadn't she been the one who'd encouraged him to see the town's possibilities? It was true that she would have liked to be involved, but that no longer appeared to be part of John's plans.

"It's wonderful!" To Claire's relief, her voice did not betray her disappointment. "When you add the shops to the carousel, it'll help make Hidden Falls a tourist attraction. I only wish . . ." She regretted the words the instant they were out of her mouth. Why was she spoiling John's announcement with her pipe dreams?

"What do you wish?"

That he loved her. That they'd have a happily-ever-after. That they'd work together on all those wonderful projects. But Claire wouldn't utter those words. Not now. Instead, she said, "That there were more jobs for the kids—not just summer jobs but something to keep them here after they graduate." If the grant for the pavilion was approved, the merry-go-round would be staffed with high school students. Steve had pointed out that "productive teenage employment" would help guarantee approval of the application. But the town needed more.

The sparkle in John's eyes seemed out of place in this discussion, particularly when combined with the solemnity of his voice. "You have to be realistic, Claire. A small town can provide only a limited number of jobs."

"I know, but . . ."

John laid his finger on his lips in the universal signal for silence. "I wasn't finished. I want to tell you about my new idea for Fairlawn."

"Have you changed your mind, and it's not going to be a luxury hotel?" Perhaps he'd decided that his affluent clientele wouldn't shop in Hidden Falls, no matter how well he renovated the textile mill.

John shook his head. "It's still going to be an exclusive resort, but there's a twist, and that depends on you."

"On me?" In the distance, Claire heard what sounded like a helicopter. That was odd. Helicopters rarely flew over Hidden Falls. She looked up but didn't see it.

"On you." John's eyes were serious. "I wondered if you'd consider continuing to teach."

For a moment, Claire was unable to breathe. Though everything he had said had been leading to this, she still felt as if she'd been hit in the solar plexus. The dream had ended. "I gather that you've found someone else to manage Fairlawn."

John tugged her to her feet. "You're doing it again, Claire." His eyes radiated warmth and something else, something that reminded Claire of the night on the hotel terrace. That was silly, of course. John was not about to kiss her. He was about to fire her. Shaking his head gently, he said, "Two plus two does not equal five."

As the helicopter came closer, Claire raised her voice to be heard over the whirl of the blades. "What am I supposed to think?" she demanded.

"You could trust me." John kept her hands in his. They were warm and firm and, if Claire were being fanciful, she would say they were loving. "You could believe that I have your best interests at heart. Didn't you tell me that you knew you'd miss teaching?" Claire nodded, unable to deny the truth. "Rick told me about a school of hotel management in Rhode Island and how they have a hotel and gourmet restaurant staffed by students. What would you think about doing that with Fairlawn?"

Claire wasn't sure what role John envisioned for her. He'd asked her to consider teaching, but she was a high school teacher, not someone qualified to join the staff of a university. "You'd need to convince one of the big schools—Cornell, Johnson and Wales, or someone like that—to let students work here."

John shook his head. "Not if the program was for high school students. Not if it was an extracurricular activity instead of an accredited course. Think of it as an extension of your Gourmet Wannabes, only the kids get paid. This would give them a chance to figure out whether or not they wanted a career in hospitality. If they did and went to a school like Cornell or J&W, they'd have a real advantage over their classmates."

Claire's mind whirled with the possibilities. She could envision a combination of classroom learning with practical experience. It would be, as John had said, an extension of the Gourmet Wannabes. It would also be a natural extension for her. It might work. Whether or not it did would depend on expectations: those of the guests and the general manager.

"The service wouldn't be perfect," Claire cautioned John as she recalled some of the meals the Gourmet Wannabes had served. "Wouldn't that bother your guests?"

John shook his head. "That's one of the changes I wanted to discuss with you. If we did this, we'd have a slightly different clientele. I thought we'd advertise it as more of a family-oriented destination." He paused and raised a brow. "So, what do you think? Is it a good idea?"

We. It hadn't been a slip of the tongue. John had used the word three times. Claire's heart began to pound with excitement. He envisioned them working together! "It's more than a good idea. It's an excellent one."

John tightened the grip on her hands. "Would you be willing to develop and run the program as well as manage Fairlawn? I know it's a lot to ask."

No other general manager. Her own school. Claire caught her breath at the prospect of having so many of her dreams come true. "It sounds wonderful," she said, shouting as the helicopter continued its approach, "but I'm not sure the logistics will work. The kids won't have much time after school once they start commuting."

John started to speak, then grinned as he glanced up at the helicopter. To Claire, it looked like every other gray and white helicopter she'd seen, but John was acting as if he recognized it.

"It looks like it wants to land here." Claire stared at the large, noisy aircraft, wondering why on earth it was hovering over the Hidden Falls High grounds.

"It does, doesn't it? C'mon, let's join the fun." John tugged on Claire's hand again, and together they ran across the grass toward the helicopter. Glinda's guests had already gathered outside the main tent and were watching the chopper descend.

By the time the blades had stopped, John and Claire had reached the front of the crowd. John kept moving, his smile widening with each step. The reason for his grin was evident a moment later when a man emerged from the cockpit.

Though Claire had never met him, the resemblance was undeniable. This was John's father.

"Hello, son." The tall, distinguished man with gray hair and the same vibrant blue eyes as his son smiled as John and Claire approached him. Though the guests were all talking at once, someone—perhaps Glinda—kept them at a distance. "I'm sorry for the delay," Henry Moreland continued, "but I figured I'd bring the news in person. Besides," he said with a wink, "I wanted to meet the woman my son plans to marry."

For the second time, Claire felt as if every breath had been squeezed out of her. *Marriage? John wanted to marry her?* She must be dreaming. But if she was, Claire hoped she'd never waken.

John's father took a step forward and extended his hand. "I'm Henry Moreland, and you must be Claire Conners."

Claire managed a nod, not trusting herself to speak. *Marriage?* She darted a glance at John. Though he smiled at his father, his expression gave no hint that he'd heard his father's declaration, much less been surprised by it. Perhaps she'd only imagined it.

As if she sensed Claire's need for support, Glinda appeared at her side and gave her hand a quick squeeze before she approached Henry Moreland.

"Good morning. Or is it afternoon?" Glinda laughed. "It doesn't matter. Whatever time it is, you've given my guests more excitement than they counted on. Some of them are convinced that your helicopter is going to be the day's entertainment, and that they're all going on rides."

The dangerous moment had passed, and Claire's brain was once more functioning. "Glinda, this is . . ."

"John's father," she said, smiling as she extended her hand in greeting.

"And you're obviously the birthday girl." Henry Moreland

shook Glinda's hand, then withdrew an envelope from his pocket. "I've brought you a present."

Glinda shook her head. "I'd be happy if you'd join the party, but no gifts are allowed."

When Henry turned to John, his son merely shrugged. "I think you'll like this one, Mrs. Conners." Henry took a step closer to Glinda and whispered something in her ear.

As Claire watched, her grandmother's expression changed from shock to sheer delight. "Thank you," she said softly. "Let's get this party started." Glinda hurried toward the platform that had been set up in the center of the tents. Henry Moreland kept pace with her, leaving Claire and John to follow in their wake.

Moving with a speed that belied her years, Glinda mounted the platform and moved toward the microphone, but she waited until Claire and John had joined her and Henry before she spoke.

"My dear, dear friends." Glinda's voice bubbled with enthusiasm. "Thank you all for coming. My granddaughter has planned an afternoon of festivities for us, but before we start, you can see that we have a gate crasher." As she nodded at Henry Moreland, the guests chuckled. "He told me that he's brought a present, not for me but for all of Hidden Falls, so I'd like to start the afternoon by introducing Henry Moreland."

Polite applause was accompanied by a definite undercurrent of speculation. "It seems strange to be back in Hidden Falls," Henry admitted. "My parents moved away when I was five, and—as you're probably aware—I haven't been back since. I plan to remedy that situation as soon as my son and his lovely partner get Fairlawn ready for guests." *Partner?* That was the first time Claire had heard herself referred to that way. "I'm hoping they'll let me come for the grand opening."

As John nodded, Henry continued. "I know you've been

worried about the town's future. I have to admit that I wasn't aware of what was happening here until a couple weeks ago. Hidden Falls wasn't, as they say, on my radar screen until John showed me the error of my ways." Henry made eye contact with several of the older men in the audience. "It's tough for someone my age to admit that he's learned from his son. Seems backwards, doesn't it?" As the audience chuckled, Claire realized where John had inherited his charisma. It was no wonder the man was so influential in state politics. Claire suspected that Henry Moreland could charm even a curmudgeon.

"You know that John is restoring my childhood home," Henry continued. "He has other plans, too, but I'll let him tell you about them when the time is right." Henry waited until the murmuring stopped. "Today I wanted to share one piece of news with you." He paused for a second, and Claire was reminded that the man was a successful trial attorney. This was probably the same dramatic pause that he used in his final summations. "Hidden Falls High School will be closed at the end of the next school year."

"Tell us something we don't know."

"Didn't need to come here in no fancy helicopter to tell us that."

The crowd began to mutter. Henry gave them a few seconds to grouse before he spoke. "You all know that. But there is one thing you don't know, because it was decided only this morning, and that's the location of the new school." The muttering ceased as everyone waited to hear Henry Moreland's next words. "The state commissioner and all three school superintendents have agreed that it will be built here, on the outskirts of Hidden Falls."

"Nice try," someone in the crowd shouted, "but the mayor told us there was no chance. Said the suits in Albany didn't like Hidden Falls."

Henry Moreland shrugged. "I've been told that I can be quite persuasive. But if you don't believe me, ask Mrs. Conners to read the document I gave her."

Glinda opened the envelope and, in a voice that was quavering with emotion, read the minutes of the meeting.

Claire turned and stared at John. This must be why he had checked his phone and watch so often. He'd been waiting for his father to give him the results of what had obviously been a special meeting of the decision makers. According to Henry Moreland, John had been the impetus behind the meeting. Claire took a deep breath as she realized what an effort that must have been. John would have had to mend breaches that were as wide as the Grand Canyon. But he'd done it, and in doing so, he'd become the miracle worker Hidden Falls needed.

Claire started to speak, but the lump in her throat kept her from uttering a sound. Hoping he'd understand, she smiled at John, and as she did, she realized that the crowd had gone wild, shouting, clapping, and cheering. It was only Claire who had been rendered speechless.

Glinda took the microphone. "Henry, I think it's safe to say that they're happy." The cheer rose another ten decibels. Glinda waited a moment, then said, "Let's give a round of applause for John too."

As the clapping and cheering continued, she turned to Claire. "He's a good man," she said softly. "I knew that the first time I met him. Why don't you marry him?"

"He hasn't asked me." Claire's words boomed across the school grounds, making her wish she could disappear beneath the platform. The microphone was still turned on, broadcasting what should have been a private conversation to the guests. Somehow they'd heard Glinda's voice over the din they were creating and had suddenly become quiet. Why hadn't she noticed that? Claire felt her face redden with embarrassment. How would she ever live this down?

"Ask her! Ask her! Ask her!" The crowd began to chant.

Claire turned and started to stumble toward the steps. She had to get out of here. She'd go home. No, that wasn't far enough. She'd disappear into one of those Central American jungles where no one would ever find her. Maybe—in a hundred years or so—she'd be able to return to Hidden Falls. Maybe by then people would have forgotten this farce. Glinda's matchmaking had gone too far. Way too far.

Claire took another step, then halted when John tugged her hand. He placed his other hand under her chin and tilted her face upward so that she was gazing into his eyes, eyes that were filled with emotion. Though they were surrounded by a hundred people, John seemed oblivious to the crowd. His hand caressed her chin, and the smile he gave her was so warm, so personal that Claire felt as if they were alone. John smiled again, then dropped slowly to one knee.

"I love you, Claire Conners," he said, his words echoing through the sound system. "Will you marry me?"

Claire stared, wanting desperately to believe her ears had not deceived her. Those were the words she'd longed to hear. This was the man she dreamed about every night, the man whose image filled her waking hours. This was the man she wanted to marry. Claire had hoped that he loved her and that one day he would say those magic words, but never, not even in her most fanciful dreams, had she imagined a proposal in such a setting.

"Are you serious?"

John nodded. "More serious than I've ever been about anything. These months with you have shown me what I want my future to be. I want a life with you as my partner, my best friend, and my wife." John tightened the grip on her hand. "I love you, Claire, and I want to spend the rest of my life with you. Will you marry me?"

"Say yes! Say yes!" The crowd surged closer.

Claire looked at the man around whom she'd woven so many dreams. His blue eyes were shining with love; his lips curved in the sweetest of smiles; his fingers entwined with hers as naturally as if they'd been meant to be together. This was what she wanted. This was what she'd dreamt of.

She smiled at the man who had the power to make her dreams come true. "I love you, John, and I can't imagine a future without you. Yes, my love, I'll marry you."

As the crowd cheered, John drew her into his arms and kissed her, and in that moment Claire knew that miracles did happen, even in Hidden Falls.

Author's Letter

Dear Reader,

I hope you enjoyed your visit to Hidden Falls, and that you're like me and are looking forward to spending many more hours there. I caught an incurable case of carousel fever in 2000 and keep finding new stories to tell about Hidden Falls, its merry-go-round and—especially—its residents.

Did your heart ache, if only a little, when you read about Rick and Josh? Did you wish someone could give them a happy ending? If so, don't worry. Their book is the next one in the series. You already know about Rick's problems. In *Stargazer* Julie Unger comes to Hidden Falls to restore the carousel. That's all she wants, but life has a way of taking unexpected turns, and Julie finds much more than she expects in the small town. Like Rick, she has a tragedy in her background, and it's one that makes him absolutely the last man she'd consider dating. Can there possibly be a happily-ever-after for them? I hope you'll get a copy of *Stargazer* when it's published in 2008 to find out what happens.

Meanwhile, if this is your first Hidden Falls romance, you might want to read *Painted Ponies* and *The Brass Ring,* both of which are currently available. They feature two of John Moreland's ancestors, twin sisters who have more than their share of problems along the path to love. Both take place in the early twentieth century when Hidden Falls was at its zenith. Although you can read them in either order, *Painted Ponies* is the first one chronologically.

As always, I look forward to hearing from you and hope you've enjoyed my stories. You're the reason I write.

Happy reading!
Amanda Harte